BUSTED

Fargo glared. There was only so much abuse he would take. "Don't lay a hand on me again."

"Or what?" Phil mockingly demanded.

"Or this." Fargo hit him. He swept his right fist up from below his waist and planted it solidly on the cocky idiot's jaw.

The blow jolted Phil onto his heels. He staggered and fell to one knee. His companion sprang to help and paid for his eagerness with a punch to the gut that doubled him over.

Thinking that was enough, Fargo swiveled to run after Draypool and the man in the dark suit, but he had taken only two steps when iron fingers locked onto his wrist and he was spun around a second time.

"I will bust you, mister!" Phil raged. Blood trickled from the left corner of his mouth, and bloodlust was in his eyes. He drew back his other hand, his fist balled. "Bust you good!"

The Colt was in Fargo's hand before any of them could blink. "Bust this," he said, and slammed the barrel against Phil's temple.

THE
TRAILSMAN
#300

BACKWOODS
BLOODBATH

by

Jon Sharpe

Ø
A SIGNET BOOK

SIGNET
Published by New American Library, a division of
Penguin Group (USA) Inc., 375 Hudson Street,
New York, New York 10014, USA
Penguin Group (Canada), 90 Eglinton Avenue East, Suite 700, Toronto,
Ontario M4P 2Y3, Canada (a division of Pearson Penguin Canada Inc.)
Penguin Books Ltd., 80 Strand, London WC2R 0RL, England
Penguin Ireland, 25 St. Stephen's Green, Dublin 2,
Ireland (a division of Penguin Books Ltd.)
Penguin Group (Australia), 250 Camberwell Road, Camberwell, Victoria 3124,
Australia (a division of Pearson Australia Group Pty. Ltd.)
Penguin Books India Pvt. Ltd., 11 Community Centre, Panchsheel Park,
New Delhi—110 017, India
Penguin Group (NZ), cnr Airborne and Rosedale Roads, Albany,
Auckland 1310, New Zealand (a division of Pearson New Zealand Ltd.)
Penguin Books (South Africa) (Pty.) Ltd., 24 Sturdee Avenue,
Rosebank, Johannesburg 2196, South Africa

Penguin Books Ltd., Registered Offices:
80 Strand, London WC2R 0RL, England

First published by Signet, an imprint of New American Library,
a division of Penguin Group (USA) Inc.

First Printing, October 2006
10 9 8 7 6 5 4 3 2 1

The first chapter of this book previously appeared in *Dakota Danger*, the two
hundred ninety-ninth volume in this series.

Copyright © Penguin Group (USA) Inc., 2006
All rights reserved

 REGISTERED TRADEMARK—MARCA REGISTRADA

Printed in the United States of America

The Trailsman

Beginnings . . . they bend the tree and they mark the man. Skye Fargo was born when he was eighteen. Terror was his midwife, vengeance his first cry. Killing spawned Skye Fargo, ruthless, cold-blooded murder. Out of the acrid smoke of gunpowder still hanging in the air, he rose, cried out a promise never forgotten.

The Trailsman they began to call him all across the West: searcher, scout, hunter, the man who could see where others only looked, his skills for hire but not his soul, the man who lived each day to the fullest, yet trailed each tomorrow. Skye Fargo, the Trailsman, the seeker who could take the wildness of a land and the wanting of a woman and make them his own.

The backwoods of Illinois, 1860—
where treachery lurks behind every tree
and a nation's fate hangs in the balance.

Prologue

The moonless night was warm and muggy. The woods fringing a farm ten miles west of Charleston, South Carolina, were as black as ink. Through those woods glided five furtive forms. They were thankful for the shroud of darkness as they neared the barn and the old stone farmhouse.

Captain Frank Colter was the leader of the five. Colter wore civilian clothes, not his uniform, as did the sergeant and three privates under his command. He was armed with a pair of short-barreled Colt revolvers, concealed under his jacket. A career soldier, Colter headed a small but special unit that reported directly to General Ira Braddock. The unit existed for one purpose and one purpose only: to ferret out insurrectionists.

Now, as Frank Colter came to a willow and hunkered behind it to survey the outbuildings, he wondered if the information he had received was genuine or if he and his men were walking into a trap.

Sentiment against the United States government was at a fever pitch and rising. A number of Southern states openly talked of seceding if the North did not give in to their demands. General Braddock had told Colter that secret arms deals with foreign powers were being brokered. Equally disturbing were reports of covert groups and societies that had sprung up in the past year or so—groups and societies whose sole purpose was to foment rebellion and bring about the

1

overthrow of the United States government by any means necessary.

The Secessionist League was one of those groups. It was rumored to have more than two hundred members across the country, among them powerful politicians and rich businessmen. Their names were kept secret, but the army had identified a handful of the members.

So far, the League had been content to send letters to the newspapers adding its voice to those demanding that the South break away from the North and form a separate government, but there were rumors, disturbing snippets picked up here and there, that the Secessionist League was plotting a diabolical act that would rock the nation.

Captain Frank Colter had been assigned to discover who the League's members were and learn what they were up to. An informer had claimed that certain top members of the League were at that very moment meeting at the farmhouse to work out the final details of their plot. The information cost two hundred dollars, but Colter considered it money well spent if it turned out to be true.

Colter was about to raise his arm to signal his men to fan out when a cough snapped his gaze to a stocky form by the barn. A man with a rifle was at the far corner, intently watching the woods on both sides.

Colter's thin lips compressed in a grim smile. The informer had not lied. Farmers did not post sentries to guard their cows. Shifting, he whispered his orders to Sergeant Pearson, who in turn relayed them to the others. As silently as stalking wolves, the four soldiers moved into position.

Captain Colter had allowed them five minutes. Then the Secessionist League would be in for an unwelcome surprise.

Colter had never thought he would live to see the day when American turned against American, when brother plotted to destroy brother. He came from a family with a tradition of proudly serving their country. His father and grandfather had been army officers, serving the Stars and Stripes with distinction. He was following in their honored footsteps.

It troubled Colter, troubled him deeply, that so many were willing to destroy the hard-won fruits of independence. Granted, no government was perfect, and there were problems. But with time and patience the two sides could work out their differences. Certain vested interests, though, did not want the differences worked out. They wanted discord. They wanted conflict. They wanted, unbelievably enough, *war*.

Colter was a soldier, but he had always believed that war should be an act of last resort. He would rather the two sides sat at a table and negotiated for years if need be, but that was not going to happen. He was too much of a realist to deny that the wellspring of hatred on both sides could end only one way.

Still, Colter would do what he could to delay that day as long as possible. To that end, he cat-footed from under the drooping boughs of the willow to a pile of freshly cut hay twenty yards from the barn.

He wished he had thought to bring a knife. He looked around but did not see a suitable rock. Resigned to clubbing the sentry with his revolver, he rose in a crouch and slid past the hay, placing each boot with care.

The sentry, with his back to Colter, was humming "Oh! Susanna." He had set the stock of a Sharps rifle on the ground and was leaning on the barrel. Suddenly he raised the rifle, but he was only stretching. He smothered a yawn, then set the stock on the ground again.

By then Colter had only ten more feet to go. He was about to straighten when a movement beyond the man alerted him to a second sentry near the farmhouse. The second one was pacing back and forth near the porch, military fashion. Lamplight spilling through a window lent the man's face a pale hue.

Tucking at the knees, Captain Colter froze. Where there were two sentries there might be more. He had to trust in his men to spot them and deal with them. If not . . . He refused to even think they would fail. Too much was at stake. Whatever the Secessionist League was plotting, it would put the antislavery faction to rout. Or so his informant had been told by a League member who talked too much while under the influence of too much ale.

The sentry by the barn started to turn. Instantly, Captain Colter flattened. The man came slowly toward him, but it was obvious by his relaxed posture that he was unaware anyone was near.

Colter tensed his legs, placed his left hand on the ground, and waited. Another six or seven steps and the sentry would be close enough. Colter glanced past him just as two dark silhouettes materialized out of the night and pounced on the man pacing in front of the porch. They overwhelmed him so quickly he had no chance to cry out.

Even so, the sentry by the barn heard something. Jerking his Sharps up, he spun and called out, "Jeb? What was that?"

Colter was in motion before the question was out of the sentry's mouth. He swept his right arm in an arc, smashing the Colt against the man's temple and felling him like a poled ox. Colter struck the prone figure again, as a precaution, then picked up the Sharps, carried it to a patch of high weeds, and hid it.

Sergeant Pearson and Private Fiske were standing over the second sentry, their revolvers glinting dully. Judging by the disjointed heap, the sentry would not awaken for many hours.

"Those were the only two, sir," Pearson whispered.

He had blond hair, cut short, and the predatory air of a hawk.

Shadows moved on either side of the farmhouse. The rest of Colter's men were taking their positions.

Motioning to Pearson, Captain Colter crept to the porch. One of the steps creaked loudly when he put his weight on it. He imitated a post, but there were no shouts of alarm. No one came to the door or peered out. Encouraged, he stalked to a window and crouched. The curtains were drawn, but an inch-wide gap enabled Colter to see into a parlor. At a circular table sat six men. Well-to-do men, by the looks of them. Leaders of the Secessionist League, according to his informant.

A tingle of excitement rippled through Colter. This was the closest he had come to nabbing those at the top. With them in custody, he stood to learn a great deal, not the least of which would be the details of their plot.

A white-haired gentleman in a white suit was addressing the others. Colter placed an ear to the pane, but he could not quite hear what the man was saying. He saw the white-haired man take a sheet of paper from a pocket and unfold it.

Time to move in, Colter decided, then abruptly stiffened. Six men were at the table, but there were seven chairs. The seventh, on the other side, was empty. *Was one of the conspirators missing?* Colter wondered. He received his answer when the front door unexpectedly opened and out stepped the seventh man, a nattily dressed broomstick with a pencil-thin mustache who was saying over his shoulder, ". . . fetch them from my saddlebags. I won't be but a minute."

The broomstick closed the door and turned to go down the steps. His eyes fell on Colter. For a few moments the man was transfixed with shock. Then he glanced toward where the sentry should be and saw

Sergeant Pearson and Private Fiske awaiting the command to close in.

The broomstick threw back his head to shout a warning.

Captain Colter was on him in a twinkling, driving his fist into the man's gut. Breath whooshed from the broomstick's lungs as he doubled over in agony. Colter slugged him again, on the jaw. Normally that was enough to drop a foe, but the man was tougher than he seemed. On his elbows and knees, dribbling spittle and wheezing for breath, he let out with a high-pitched keen: "Federals!"

How he knew, Captain Colter couldn't say. The next moment the man's right hand rose. In it he clutched a derringer.

The boom of Sergeant Pearson's revolver heralded a shriek and a fervid curse as the broomstick, severely wounded, scrabbled toward the front door to get back inside. He pointed the derringer at Colter and hissed, "Damn you Yankees all to hell!"

Colter shot him through the head. As the body crumpled, shouts broke out inside. The League members were in an uproar. The curtains parted, and the white-haired man in the white suit took one look at Colter, whirled, and ran.

"Is the back door covered?" Captain Colter shouted. Pearson replied that it was.

Colter sprang to the door as the window he had been standing next to dissolved under a hail of lead. He flung the door open and beheld a League member, aiming a revolver, midway down a narrow hall. Colter darted aside as the muzzle spat lead and smoke. He heard Private Fiske cry out sharply.

More shots erupted from the rear of the farmhouse, laced with yells and oaths. After that, silence fell.

Captain Colter risked a peek inside. The hallway was empty now, but a commotion farther back suggested the conspirators were up to something.

A boot scuffed the porch, and Sergeant Pearson bounded to the other side of the doorway. His back to the wall, he whispered, "Fiske was wounded in the arm, but it's not serious, sir."

"We have them boxed in," Colter declared with a confidence he did not feel. His men had the doors covered, but there were not enough of them to cover all the ground-floor windows as well.

"Should I call on them to surrender, sir?" Sergeant Pearson asked.

"I will," Captain Colter said. Raising his voice, he identified himself, adding, "My men have the house surrounded. You would be well advised to throw down your arms and come out with your hands over your heads!"

"Go to hell!" came a taunt in a distinct Southern drawl.

"Northern trash!" another cried defiantly.

Sergeant Pearson glanced at Colter. "Just give the order, sir, and we will rush them."

But Colter did no such thing. There was no telling how many League members were inside. There might be more that he had not seen.

Glass tinkled, and an upstairs window burst outward. A rifle spat, but its target, Private Fiske, had gone to ground behind a rosebush.

"Maybe we should burn them out, sir," Sergeant Pearson proposed.

"We want them alive if possible—remember?" Captain Colter said. The key phrase was "if possible." Clearing his throat, he yelled, "You, in the house! Can you hear me in there?"

After a bit, someone—Colter suspected it was the white-haired gentleman—responded, "We can hear you just fine. What do you want?"

"To avoid bloodshed," Captain Colter said. "Give yourselves up and I promise no harm will come to you."

7

A cold chuckle greeted the offer. "You would like that, wouldn't you? But mark my words. You will not get your hands on a single one of us. We will gladly die rather than let you take us."

Colter had been afraid of that. Fanatics and politics made for a rabid mix. Somehow he must convince them that they should deny their loyalty to a cause they valued more than life itself.

"Did you hear me?" the man demanded when Colter did not answer soon enough to suit him.

"I believe you," Colter shouted. "But don't do anything rash! We can talk this out!"

"Like hell!"

A minute passed. Then every window on the ground floor abruptly crashed into shards. Chairs had been hurled against them. Through the windows scrambled the occupants. Shots were exchanged. Shouts added to the bedlam.

Colter had been right. There were more than six, and they were making a frantic break for the woods. He ran to the end of the porch in time to see several fleeing shadows. One man turned and fired. Colter returned lead for lead. The man missed. Colter did not.

The white suit gave Colter a clue who it was. Vaulting over the rail, Colter ran and covered him. "Don't try anything."

The white-haired man coughed and spat blood. His eyes opened and could not seem to focus, but finally they did. His face twisted in a hateful grimace. "You have murdered me, you son of a bitch."

"What are you planning?" Captain Colter asked. "What is the Secessionist League up to?"

A contemptuous laugh gurgled from the man's throat and with it, a copious amount of blood. "You would like that, wouldn't you? For me to turn traitor against the cause I believe in?" He had more to say, but a violent coughing fit interfered.

Colter squatted and took hold of the man's shoulders. "Don't die on me, damn it! I need to know."

A smirk curled the man's mouth. "It's too late for me. I feel my life ebbing. But maybe I will give you a clue."

Suspecting the clue would be worthless, Captain Colter said, "I'm listening."

"We don't have far to go," the man said, and cackled as if it were the funniest utterance ever made. More blood flowed from both his mouth and his nose. He choked. He sputtered. Then he was still.

"Is he gone?" Sergeant Pearson asked.

"Yes."

"What was that he said about not having far to go?"

"I wish to heaven I knew," Captain Colter said in frustration. The raid had not worked out as planned. He was no closer to the truth, and countless lives were at stake. He summed up his sentiments with a simple "Damn."

1

Skye Fargo was having one of those nights when Lady Luck sat on his shoulder. He had won two hundred dollars at poker, bucked the tiger at faro and won sixty-seven dollars more, and was now back at the poker table facing a stack of chips in the pot that promised to add five hundred to his poke if he won.

The only thing better than a winning streak was a willing woman, and Fargo's luck had held in that regard, too. A dove by the name of Saucy had taken a shine to him earlier that night when he strolled in through the batwings. She was like a she-bear drawn to honey—and he was the honey.

Miss Saucy McBride was quite an eyeful. Red hair cascaded in curls to bare white shoulders as smooth as alabaster. She had an oval face distinguished by full, upturned lips that appeared as succulent as ripe cherries. A scarlet dress clung to her full figure as if painted on. But it was her eyes that most interested Fargo—hazel pools of desire mixed with a healthy sense of humor.

At the moment, Saucy was perched on Fargo's lap with one arm around his neck and the other resting on his thigh. She was making small circles on his leg with the tips of her fingers. Fargo wanted to throw her to the sawdust-covered floor and have her right there, but there was the matter of winning the five hundred dollars.

Four other players were at the same table. One had already folded. Another was a mousey store clerk who bet only when he had a sure hand, which always turned out to be an especially good one.

The third player, a chunky bank teller partial to cheap, foul-smelling cigars, played like a bull in a china shop. He bet practically every hand and bluffed as often as he held good cards. There was no predicting him, although Fargo had noticed that the last two times the teller had bluffed, he removed his cigar from his mouth and tapped it in the ashtray before betting.

The fourth player was cut from a whole different cloth. Hale Tilton was a gambler by profession. He favored a black jacket and pants, with a frilled white shirt. A wide-brimmed black hat was tillted low over his eyes so no one could read his expression. He, too, was unpredictable, although slightly less so in that he did not bluff as often as the teller. When he did, it was because he sensed weakness in the others' hands.

The teller was about to bet. He took his cigar from his mouth, tapped it on the ashtray, and pushed in fifty dollars.

"Interesting," Hale Tilton said, and added fifty of his own.

It was Fargo's turn. He had two queens, a king, an eight, and a three. Only a queen and the three were the same suit. It was not a great hand, but it had potential. He debated discarding the king, eight, and three and asking for two cards, then decided to discard only the eight and the three. But first he had to bet.

Fargo was fairly certain the teller was bluffing. The store clerk had at least a pair of jacks or he would not have opened. Hale Tilton might have a good hand or he might be counting on the draw. Either and all ways, Fargo was not about to bow out with a pair of queens. He added fifty dollars and asked for two cards.

The player who had folded was dealing. Another townsman, he wore a brown jacket and a bowler, and he could never seem to sit still. He was forever fidgeting. Fargo took it to be because the man had a nervous temperament, but now, as the man flicked cards to the store clerk, Fargo saw something that set his blood to boiling. If there was one thing he could not stand, it was a cheat.

Hale Tilton, in the act of stacking his chips, froze for an instant with his fingers poised over the table. Then slowly, almost sadly, he lowered his hand and said softly, "Well, well, well."

"What's the matter, Tilton?" the dealer asked with a smirk. "Not getting the cards you need?"

"Oh, I have no complaints," the gambler responded. "Not about the cards, anyway. It's simpletons who get my dander up. They mistakenly think I'm as simple-minded as they are."

"Surely you're not referring to any of us?" the teller demanded, his cigar clenched in a corner of his mouth.

"Not you, no," Hale Tilton said. He focused on Fargo. "Do you want to do this or would you rather I did the honors?"

Fargo had played the gambler a few times before. He did not know Tilton well, but as rumor had it, he was fairly honest, for a cardsharp, and had a reputation as a gent who should not be crossed. "Be my guest," Fargo said, and leaned back.

Hale Tilton glanced from the dealer to the store clerk and back again. "It always amazes me when peckerwoods try."

"Try what?" the clerk nervously asked.

"In case you have forgotten, I gamble for a living. From Mississippi riverboats to prairie hovels to log saloons along the Columbia River, I have seen it all, done it all, where cards are involved."

The dealer snickered. "Are you bragging or complaining?"

"I am making a point, Niles," Hale Tilton said. He pushed his chair back and placed his forearms on the table, and if anyone besides Fargo noticed the slight metallic scrape Tilton's right wrist made, they did not show it. "I've seen trimmed cards, cards with sliced corners, cards with bumps. I've seen holdouts of all kinds. Up the sleeve, in vest pockets, in belts. I've seen card cheats use special spectacles to read phosphorescent ink on the backs of cards. I've seen men use bugs."

Fargo had been in a saloon in Kansas when a man was caught using a bug. Made of steel and shaped like a money clip with two sharp ends, the bug was jammed under a table and held cards the bug's owner palmed until they were needed. The man in Kansas had been fortunate. Instead of stretching his neck, as was customary, the other players tarred and feathered him.

Niles glowered at the gambler. "There are a thousand and one ways to cheat, Tilton. What of it?"

"Usually only professionals mark cards and use holdouts," Hale Tilton remarked. "Amateurs deal from the bottom of the deck or play with a friend and set up secret signals, or both." The gambler stared squarely at Niles. "How you two expected to get away with it is beyond me."

"I don't know what you're talking about," Niles huffed. He slid his right hand close to the edge of the table, and to his open brown jacket.

Tilton switched his hard stare to the store clerk. "And you, Weaver. Why would you try it? Don't I always play fair with you boys when I visit Kansas City?"

Weaver paled and looked at Niles, who angrily demanded, "Are you accusing the two of us of cheating? Of working together to fleece a few hands?"

"Yes, that is exactly what I am saying," Hale Tilton said. "But you are free to prove me wrong. Turn over your cards, Mr. Weaver, and show us what Mr. Niles has dealt you."

Fargo patted Saucy on the fanny and bobbed his chin. A veteran of her trade, she understood immediately; she rose and moved well away from the table. Fargo lowered his right hand and hooked his thumb in his belt next to his Colt.

Weaver was not especially brave, but he knew his poker. "I am not required to show my hand until the betting is done. That's the rule."

"No one else is going to bet," the gambler said quietly.

"Even so," Weaver said, his voice rising, "I'm not turning my cards over, and that's final."

"You *are* turning them over," Hale Tilton insisted, "or this will be your final day on earth."

Nearby players and patrons had overheard. A current of hushed voices rippled through the room. All eyes turned to their table. The more prudent sidled elsewhere to avoid taking a stray slug.

Fargo happened to notice one man who did not. Another townsman, he sported bushy sideburns and, like Niles, wore a bowler. The man had been idly watching their game. Fargo had not thought anything of it until now. He realized that the man was standing behind Hale Tilton, but to one side, where Tilton was less apt to notice.

A conviction came over Fargo that there was more to Niles's and Weaver's shenanigans. On a hunch, he casually shifted in his chair, and sure enough, another townsman was behind him. It set him to wondering why they had let him win so much. Maybe he was imagining things. But then, it was his habit to keep his cards flat on the table and slide them close to the edge before taking a quick peek.

The man behind him had not been able to see his cards.

The bank teller removed his cigar and jabbed the lit end at Niles. "Is what he says true? Have you and Weaver been cheating us?"

"Of course not, Sam," Niles said unconvincingly.

"Because if you have," the teller went on, "it stands to reason this isn't the first time."

Niles colored the same shade as a beet and snapped, "I tell you it's not true! Why in hell don't you believe me?"

Sam jabbed the air with his cigar again. "Because it explains how you manage to win so often on days that me and some of the other boys get paid. Or didn't you think any of us would notice?"

"I don't have to sit here and take this!" Niles declared, and started to rise. He stopped when Hale Tilton's right arm rose and extended in his direction, Tilton's fingers bent slightly back.

"You are not going anywhere until your friend turns over the cards you dealt him," the gambler said in a low tone pregnant with menace.

Weaver was squirming in his chair like a chipmunk on a hot rock. "Niles? What do I do?"

"You don't turn over the cards and you keep your damn mouth shut." Niles gazed expectantly around the room, but if he was hoping for support from any of the onlookers, he was disappointed. No one was willing to intervene. Cheating at cards, like stealing a horse, was a serious offense.

"The cards, Mr. Weaver," Hale Tilton said quietly.

Trembling like an aspen leaf in a brisk breeze, Weaver reached for his cards but stopped at a sharp cry from Niles.

"Don't you touch them, damn you! He has no right to make you! We will forget about this hand. Everyone can take their money from the pot, and that will be that."

"No, it will not." The gambler slowly rose. "My patience has a limit, gentlemen. I strongly suggest you do as I have asked."

Without being obvious, Fargo was keeping an eye on the townsman behind Tilton and the townsman behind him. The gambler, preoccupied with Niles and Weaver, had not noticed them.

"You can go to hell!" Niles blustered.

"After you," Hale Tilton said.

"Someone send for the marshal!" Niles was clutching at a legal straw. "He'll put a stop to this nonsense."

No one moved, nor offered to go. The bartender brought his hands up from under the bar. He was holding a shotgun, but he did not point it at their table. He was content to let the confrontation play itself out without interfering unless he absolutely had to.

Fargo edged his right hand closer to his Colt. Experience had taught him that when the explosion came, it would be swift and brutal.

Hale Tilton leaned across the table. With his left hand he turned over the cards in question. "Just as I thought."

Four aces and a king lay there for all to see. Too late, Weaver snatched them and clutched them to his chest. "It wasn't my idea," he said.

"Hush, damn you!" Niles fumed. "He can't prove anything if you keep your fool mouth shut!"

"Who needs to?" the gambler asked. "What will it be? Parade you down the street tied to a rail?"

"I would like to see someone try," Niles snarled, and made as if to leave. As he turned, his hand darted under his jacket.

A flick of Hale Tilton's wrist, and just like that a nickel-plated derringer gleamed in the lamplight. The *click* of the hammer was loud enough for Fargo and those at the table to hear. But that did not deter Niles.

His arm came out from under his jacket, and so did a Remington.

"Kill the son of a bitch, boys!" Niles cried.

Hale Tilton shot him.

The townsman behind Tilton and the townsman behind Fargo clawed at concealed revolvers. In a heartbeat Fargo was out of his chair with his Colt level. He sent a slug into the man behind the gambler, whirled, and banged off a second shot, all so fast that to the onlookers the two shots sounded as one.

The townsman behind Fargo did not go down. He staggered against the wall, regained his balance, and brought up a Smith and Wesson.

Fargo never did like backshooters. He shot the man in the chest, not once but twice, and at each cracking retort, holes appeared in the townsman's store-bought shirt. The man was dead before his face smacked the floorboards.

Gun smoke hung in the air. Niles was sprawled on his back with a new hole between his eyes. The townsman behind Tilton was on his side, groaning and mewing about his shoulder being broken.

"I'm obliged for the help," the gambler said.

Fargo scanned the onlookers. None were disposed to avenge the fallen. He started to reload, saying, "There is no shortage of jackasses in this world."

Nodding, Hale Tilton grinned. "If a man can't cheat worth a damn, he should take up knitting."

Now it was Fargo who grinned, but the grin evaporated when what he took to be another townsman came striding purposefully toward them. Quickly, Fargo replaced the last spent cartridge and twirled the Colt so the muzzle pointed at the newcomer. "That's far enough, mister. I have plenty of peas left."

The man stopped. Smiling suavely, he doffed a derby and said with a slight twang, "I assure you, sir, I mean you no harm. Quite the contrary. Your marvelous display has confirmed the reports we have received about you."

"What the hell are you jabbering about?"

"It's quite simple, really." The man's smile widened. "My associates and I would like to hire you to kill someone."

2

Skye Fargo did not hire out his gun to kill. He was a tracker, a scout, a frontiersman. He was fond of cards, whiskey, and women, although not necessarily in that order. He was prone to wander, spurred by an unquenchable yearning to see what lay over the next horizon. He had killed before, many times, but always when it had to be done, when his life or the lives of others hung in the balance, when it was survive or die.

"I'm not a hired assassin," he said curtly.

"Did I give the impression I thought you were?" the man rejoined. "If so, I apologize. Perhaps I phrased my praise in the wrong vein. It need not be you who does the killing." He paused. "We are interested in you primarily for your tracking ability, which we hear is outstanding."

Fargo studied the man anew; his clothes were nicely tailored, a gold watch chain hung from a fine vest, his polished shoes shone. This man was not the sort who usually frequented watering holes like the Hitch Rail.

"Mind if I buy you a drink and you and I discuss our proposal?"

Hale Tilton had been listening. "Go ahead if you want," he said to Fargo. "I'll explain things to the marshal when he shows up."

"If he needs me I'll be over there." Fargo pointed at an empty corner table. "After you," he said to the dandy with the gold watch. "I'll join you in a minute." He scooped up his winnings.

A crowd was gathering. Word had spread, and people were drifting in from the street to see the bodies. Someone began bellowing about fetching a sawbones to tend the man with the broken shoulder.

"My name is Draypool, by the way," the dandy said, offering his hand as Fargo came over. "Arthur Draypool. I hail from Illinois."

"You're a long way from home."

"And have been for the past several weeks, searching for you," Draypool revealed. "You were hard to find. You never stayed in one place long enough for me to catch up to you, until now."

Fargo tried to motion to the bartender for a bottle, but the barkeep had joined those around the dead and wounded.

"Have a seat," Draypool said, indicating a chair next to his.

Instead, Fargo sat in a different chair, with his back to the entrance.

"What's wrong with this one?" Draypool asked.

"I've made a few enemies," Fargo said.

"My word! Are you saying that someone might walk up to you and shoot you in the back without any warning? I can't imagine what that must be like. It would wear me down, always having to look over my shoulder."

"You get used to it," Fargo said, which was not entirely true. "Enough about me. Why are you here?"

"Where to begin?" Arthur Draypool mused aloud. "Perhaps by asking whether you have ever been to the glorious state of Illinois?"

"What's so glorious about it?"

"Obviously you have never been there. I wasn't born in Illinois, but I'm proud to be an Illinoisan. Proud to be a citizen of the United States. Proud to be an American."

Fargo leaned back and folded his arms across his chest. Draypool reminded him of certain politicians he had met.

"Illinois has been a state for only about forty years, but I predict great things for her in the decades to come."

"Her?" Fargo said.

"It is quite common to use the female gender when referring to things like boats, guns, and states. Davy Crockett, if you'll recall, referred to his rifle as Old Betsy. What do you call yours?"

"A Henry."

"But that's the name of the manufacturer. Haven't you ever referred to, say, a steamboat or a canoe as 'she' or 'her'?"

"Only if I was really drunk," Fargo said, "and if I did, I was so drunk I don't remember."

"We're straying from the point," Draypool said in mild exasperation. "Namely, that Illinois is a fine state, with great prospects. Especially in the political realm. Surely even you have heard about the famous debates between Abraham Lincoln and Stephen A. Douglas?"

Fargo did not miss the "even you." Evidently Draypool viewed him as a buckskin-clad bumpkin. "There was a debate?" he asked in sham ignorance.

"My word, man! Don't you ever read a newspaper?" The Illinoisan clucked like an irritated hen. "Surely you at least know that Abraham Lincoln is running for president this year?"

"He is?" Fargo was thankful for his years of experience at poker. Otherwise he would have given himself away.

Draypool's mouth fell open. Then his brow knit and a quizzical expression came over him. "Wait. You're mocking me, aren't you?"

"Why would I do that?"

For all of fifteen seconds Arthur Draypool sat in thoughtful silence. Then he said, "Fair enough. I suppose I deserved to be put in my place. It was not polite of me to treat you as I did. Please accept my sincere apologies."

"When will you get to that point you mentioned?" Fargo noticed a commotion over at the batwings, and in hurried the town marshal with a deputy in tow.

"Are all plainsmen so straightforward?" Draypool asked, but he did not wait for a reply. "Very well. As I have mentioned, Illinois has great things in store. She grows by leaps every year as more and more people flock to her from back east. Ten years from now she will be one of the leading states in the areas of commerce and culture."

"Your point," Fargo reiterated when Draypool took a breath.

"Please be patient. You see, right now much of Illinois is wilderness. We still have our share of Indian troubles, even though we defeated the Fox and Sauk tribes in the Black Hawk War. We also have our share of white troublemakers, riffraff who live by the gun and the knife. Outlaws and cutthroats who think God granted them the right to rob and kill as they see fit."

"It's the same most everywhere along the frontier," Fargo said, "and worse west of the Mississippi River."

"True," Draypool conceded. "And it is up to decent, law-abiding people everywhere to put an end to the depredations. Whether white or red, those who steal and plunder must be put to the noose or spend the rest of their natural lives behind bars."

"You should run for governor," Fargo said. He meant it as a jest, but Draypool beamed and puffed out his chest.

"Why, thank you. I just might one day. For the moment I am content to do what I can to rid Illinois of her unsavory elements." He paused. "One of the worst is known as the Sangamon River Monster."

"Is it a ferocious frog? Or a bass that has taken to

climbing out of the river and swallowing people as they stroll by?"

Arthur Draypool blinked, then uttered a brittle little laugh. "That's quite the sense of humor you have. But no, the Sangamon River Monster is neither frog nor fish. It is a man. The most vile human being to walk the face of the earth."

"I can think of a few others who can lay claim to the honor."

"Do they raid isolated farms and put them to the torch? Do they torture and mutilate entire families? Men, women, and children? I doubt there is anyone, anywhere, half as vicious as the Sangamon River Monster."

"Ever hear of the Apaches?"

"Of course. But you expect it of them. There exists a natural animosity between the white man and the red man. They are primitive savages who live in squalid dwellings made of animal hides, whereas the white man embodies the highest sense of refinement and civilization."

Fargo considered slugging him. "Have I mentioned that I've lived with a few of those primitive savages?"

"You don't say?" Draypool realized he had made a mistake and tried to make amends. "Don't get me wrong, sir. I am not one of those who looks down his nose at everyone and everything red. One of my best friends when I was growing up was an Indian boy. Be that as it may—"

"What was his name?" Fargo interrupted.

"I beg your pardon?"

"What was the name of your friend?"

Draypool coughed and took an interest in the arrival of the doctor. Finally he said, "I can't recall the Indian boy's name at the moment. You must understand, it has been quite a while since I saw him last."

"I savvy perfectly," Fargo assured him.

"None of this is relevant anyway. The Sangamon River Monster is white. For ten years he has terrorized central Illinois. It's time we put a stop to it. That is where you come in."

Fargo dearly needed a drink, but the bartender was still over by the bodies. "What's so special about me? Don't you have trackers in Illinois? Or bloodhounds?"

"Permit me to place things in their proper perspective." Draypool rested both elbows on the table. "As I have mentioned, Illinois is largely backwoods country. Forests as they were ages before the first white man set foot on this continent. Woodland so thick, many travel by foot instead of on horseback."

"Mountain men aren't the only ones who like to tell tall tales," Fargo said.

"You think I exaggerate?" Draypool shook his head. "You will see for yourself when you come to Illinois."

"Hold that notion." Fargo stood and went to the bar. Most everyone else was over listening to the tin star question the gambler. The few still at the counter paid him no mind as he swung up and over and dropped lightly to the other side. He selected a bottle of Monongahela from a row of bottles of all shapes and sizes. Placing it on the bar, he was about to vault back over when the twin muzzles of a shotgun blossomed in front of his face.

"I trust you were fixing to pay for that."

Fargo glared at the bartender. "Harve, have you ever known me not to make good?"

"I wish all my customers were as dependable as you," Harve Bennet answered, and laughed. "Admit it. I about made you wet yourself."

"Wishful thinking. I saw you in the mirror." Fargo had done no such thing, but he would not give Harve the satisfaction.

"Dang. You're like a damned hawk. You never miss

a cussed thing. What would I have to do to be more like you?"

"Spend ten years roaming the prairie and the mountains," Fargo said, hefting the whiskey bottle, "and lose fifty pounds."

Harve placed a beefy hand on his bulging middle. "That was uncalled for. I can't help it if pouring drinks doesn't give a man much muscle."

Fargo dug in a pocket and slapped down the coins needed to pay for the rotgut. "Here. Treat yourself to a cow." He smirked all the way to the table.

"As I was saying," Arthur Draypool said the moment Fargo sat down, "the Sangamon River Monster's reign of terror must end. Which is why my associates and I are willing to pay a substantial sum for your services."

A long swig of whiskey did wonders for Fargo's disposition. Smacking his lips, he said, "Trackers and bloodhounds, remember?"

"Of course we have them. Backwoodsmen are as common as fleas, and bragging about their hounds is their favorite pastime. Time and again trackers and dogs have gone out after the Monster, and time and again they have not returned, or returned without finding him."

"Why haven't I ever heard of him?" Fargo rarely read newspapers, but he did keep up with saloon gossip, and most everything worthwhile found mention eventually. It was how he had heard about the Lincoln-Douglas debates, and that Abraham Lincoln was the Republican candidate for president. Politics never interested him, but the next election promised to be a corker. It was dividing the country into pro-slavery and antislavery camps, with each camp throwing insults and threats at the other. If things kept on as they were, bloodshed was bound to result.

Draypool was talking. "Why should you have

heard of him? The Sangamon River Monster is not well known outside of Illinois's borders. Probably because he's white. If he were an Indian, newspapers all over the country would carry accounts of his atrocities."

The man had a point there, Fargo admitted. Newspapers reveled in reports of massacres and outrages committed by the red race, usually to illustrate why it was the white man's duty to place all of them on white-run reservations where they could learn white ways and live like whites forever after.

"Give the Monster a few more years," Draypool said, "and I warrant he will garner a lot more attention. But we don't want that. Illinois does not need the adverse publicity. It will deter people from moving there." He uttered a deep sigh. "The group I represent is dedicated to Illinois's betterment. The Monster is a detriment we can do without."

Fargo treated himself to another swig of whiskey. The man sure was fond of big words, but there was no denying he cared about Illinois and the folks in it. "When was the last time anyone tried to track this Monster of yours?"

"Two and a half months ago. He wiped out a family of five near Decatur. Three of the best trackers in the state went after him and never came back."

"What's his name?" Fargo did not recall it being mentioned.

"No one knows. Neither his name, nor where he is from, nor why he does what he does." Draypool clasped his hands in eager appeal. "What do you say? Will you accept our proposal and end his killing spree?"

Fargo hesitated. Illinois was a long way from his usual haunts, and eastern forests were nothing like western forests.

Arthur Draypool played his trump card. "As an added inducement, I am authorized to pay you a handsome sum. Half now, and half when the Monster has been brought to bay."

"How handsome a sum?" Fargo began to chug more whiskey, and nearly choked on the reply.

"How does ten thousand dollars sound?"

3

Ten thousand dollars. Fargo could not get the amount out of his head. It was more than he had ever had at any one time in his life. The smart thing to do would be to squirrel most of it away for his waning years. That made the most sense. But knowing him, he would do what he always did with a windfall: he would spend it on the three things he liked most in life and have none left by the time he was done indulging. Besides, there was a certain high-stakes poker game in Denver in a couple of months. Ten grand to sit in, and the winner always walked away with upwards of half a million.

"Do we have an accord, then?" Arthur Draypool asked.

They were outside the Hitch Rail. A few yards away was a genuine hitch rail, lined with horses. The street was uncommonly busy for that time of night. It was past eleven P.M., yet pedestrians and riders went briskly about their nocturnal business.

"We have a deal," Fargo confirmed, and held out his hand.

"You can't possibly imagine how grateful we are." Draypool's shake was weak, his palm wet with sweat even though the temperature had dropped to below seventy degrees.

Fargo watched the Illinoisan walk off. They had

agreed to meet the next morning at seven at Draypool's hotel. By eight they would be on their way east.

About to go back inside, Fargo paused. The street was not well lit, but there was enough light spilling from windows that he clearly saw a man emerge from the recessed doorway of a butcher shop and follow in Draypool's steps. It seemed innocent enough, and Fargo would not have thought anything of it except that the butcher shop was closed, its doorway in shadow. The man who stepped out of it, therefore, had been concealed there, waiting for just that moment.

Kansas City, like most cities and towns along the mighty Mississippi River, crawled with what newspaper editors liked to refer to as "the criminal element." Pickpockets were a plague. Robberies were so common they rarely merited mention. Only more serious crimes, like murder, were splashed over the front pages.

Yet another reason for Fargo, upon seeing the man in the dark suit follow Draypool, to leap to the commonsense conclusion that the man intended to separate Draypool from his money, or do him harm, or both.

Fargo frowned. Saucy McBride was waiting inside to attend to unfinished business, but he could not very well ignore the threat to Draypool. Hoping Saucy would understand if he kept her waiting, Fargo shadowed the shadower. It was not hard to do in the crowded street.

Fargo thought, with some annoyance, that Draypool had brought this on himself. The man's expensive clothes and hat, the gold watch, the costly shoes, practically screamed that Draypool had money, a lot of money, and that he was likely to carry a wad of bills well worth stealing.

It was four blocks to the Sunflower, a new hotel that catered to those with Draypool's refined tastes. Fargo had never been inside, but he had been told that the lobby boasted a crystal chandelier, plush carpet, a mahogany front desk, and brass fixtures. The rooms cost more than those at any other hotel—rooms so luxurious that each had a sterling silver chamber pot.

Arthur Draypool was strolling along without a care in the world. Now and then he slowed to gaze in store windows or gaze at the stars or gaze at people passing by, but not once did he think to gaze behind him, which was typical for an Easterner. They always assumed places like Kansas City were the same as cities in more civilized parts of the country, relatively safe.

To be fair, even Eastern cities had their share of two-legged wolves, but the farther west one went, the more violent the wolves were prone to be. As Draypool would, no doubt, soon find out.

Fargo quickened his pace. The man in the dark suit was matching Draypool stride for stride, and as yet not ready to close in. Fargo figured the man would wait until they came to a section of street where there were fewer lights.

Draypool passed a dance hall. Every window blazed, and tinny music blared to the heavens. A constant flow of men and women entering or leaving forced Draypool to slow yet again and thread through them.

The man in the dark suit had to do the same. As he passed under the large lamps on either side of the entrance, Fargo got his first clear glimpse of his quarry, and he was surprised by what he saw.

The would-be robber did not have the seedy, predatory air of most of his kind. In fact, he looked perfectly respectable. His suit was clean and pressed, and while not immaculately tailored like Draypool's, it was a cut above what most other men were wearing. To Fargo it indicated the man was good at his illegal trade. Fargo did not see evidence of a weapon, but the robber was bound to be a walking armory.

A woman came out of the dance hall. She was looking down and did not notice the man in the dark suit until she nearly collided with him. Startled, she drew up short, and the man doffed his hat and said something that brought a smile. He let her go on past before resuming his stalk of Draypool.

Now Fargo had seen everything. A gentleman footpad. *And why not?* he asked himself. He knew men who would knife or shoot others at the slightest provocation, but who were as polite as polite could be the rest of the time.

Fargo reached the dance hall. The music was so loud it nearly drowned out the babble of voices. He tucked his chin to his chest so if the man in the dark suit happened to look back, it would give the impression that Fargo had no interest in him.

Just then, out spilled a rowdy crowd of ten to fifteen people. Joking and laughing and having a grand time, they enveloped Fargo like a human cloud, and before he knew it, he was surrounded and hemmed in. He tried to press through them, but a brunette in an invitingly tight dress and a floral hat hooked her arm through his and held on.

"Whoa there, handsome! What's your hurry?"

Fargo smiled and tried to pry her arm loose. "I have something to do." But she would not let go.

"It can wait. My name is Nanette. What would yours be?"

"I don't have time for this." Fargo glimpsed the man in the dark suit, the gap between them widening with every second of delay.

"Oh, posh." Nanette squeezed tighter and brazenly pecked him on the cheek. "I've taken a shine to you. What do you say to the two of us going off to have a few drinks together?"

In Fargo's estimation she had already had enough. The whiskey on her breath was enough to gag a mule. "I really must be on my way," he insisted.

"What's the matter? Aren't I pretty enough for

you? I'll have you know men pay me compliments all the time."

Fargo didn't doubt it. She had nice eyes and a lovely mouth and a body most men would drool over, but once again he gently tried to pry her hand off. She dug her fingers into his sleeve, and he applied more force, none too gently twisting her wrist until she had no choice but to release him.

"Owww!" Nanette squealed, and flushed with anger. "What's the big idea? A girl tries to be friendly and you break her arm off!"

To explain would be pointless. Fargo started to go around her when a heavy hand fell on his shoulder and he was spun halfway around.

"Where the hell do you think you're going? That was no way to treat a lady. Apologize or else."

Confronting Fargo were two men in their early twenties. Like Nanette, they had been drinking heavily and were at that stage where belligerence replaced reason. "This has nothing to do with you," he said.

"That's where you're wrong, mister," the shorter of the pair declared. He was built like a block of wood, with shoulders a bull would envy. "Nan is our friend, and we don't take kindly to her being mistreated."

The rest of their party had stopped and were awaiting developments. If Fargo wasn't careful, he would have a fight on his hands. Not that he minded a good, healthy brawl, but he had Draypool to think of. Touching a hand to his hat brim, he said to Nanette, "I hope I didn't hurt you." He turned to go, only to have the same heavy hand clamp on his arm.

"That's not good enough," the bull-shouldered youth said. "Not by a long shot." He slurred a few of his words. "Say you are sorry and mean it."

"You tell him, Phil!" Nanette cried.

Fargo glared. There was only so much abuse he would take. "Don't lay a hand on me again."

"Or what?" Phil mockingly demanded.

32

"Or this." Fargo hit him. He swept his right fist up from below his waist and planted it solidly on the cocky idiot's jaw.

The blow jolted Phil onto his heels. He staggered and fell to one knee. His companion sprang to help and paid for his eagerness with a punch to the gut that doubled him over.

Thinking that was enough, Fargo swiveled to run after Draypool and the man in the dark suit, but he had taken only two steps when iron fingers locked onto his wrist and he was spun around a second time.

"I will bust you, mister!" Phil raged. Blood trickled from the left corner of his mouth, and bloodlust was in his eyes. He drew back his other hand, his fist balled. "Bust you good!"

The Colt was in Fargo's hand before any of them could blink. "Bust this," he said, and slammed the barrel against Phil's temple. Phil collapsed in an unconscious pile. The rest turned to ice. "Anyone else?"

Nanette put her hands on her hips and stepped up to him, eliciting gasps from a few of her friends. "You had no call to do that! Pulling a gun on someone who is unarmed! I have half a mind to fetch the marshal."

Fargo had half a mind to throw her over his knee and spank her, but he settled for twirling the Colt into his holster with a flourish to impress her friends and convince them they were better off dropping the matter. "Yes, you do," he said, and headed up the street before she figured out what he meant.

Arthur Draypool and the man in the dark suit were nowhere to be seen.

Cursing under his breath, Fargo broke into a jog. The slap of his boots and the jangle of his spurs forewarned most of those in front of him, and they took one glance and got out of his way. He covered two blocks with fewer lights and ripe opportunity before he spied the skulker in the dark suit. Fargo immediately slowed to a walk.

33

Fargo wondered if maybe he was wrong. The man was the same distance between Draypool as before, and showed no inclination to get closer. Then Draypool stopped to admire a new carriage passing by, and the man in the dark suit stopped and pretended to be interested in the window of a general store he was passing. When Draypool went on, so did his shadow.

Up ahead the Sunflower appeared. It was set back from the street, along a tree-lined pathway. The moment Arthur Draypool turned up the path, the man in the dark suit halted and slid a hand under his jacket.

Instantly, Fargo's hand was on his Colt. But the man did not pull a gun. He produced what appeared to be a pencil and a small notebook and scribbled in it after consulting his watch.

"What in hell is going on?" Fargo wondered aloud. The man's behavior was a complete mystery.

A doorman admitted Draypool. As soon as the door closed behind him, the man in the dark suit replaced the pencil and notebook in an inside pocket and resumed walking in a leisurely fashion past the hotel.

Curiosity compelled Fargo to follow. He had to find out what the man was up to. At the next corner they turned right. At the corner after that, left. Another hotel, the Imperial, was the man's destination. It catered to those who liked a decent room for a decent price. Fargo had stayed there a couple of times himself. The rooms were plain, the furnishings simple, but a man could enjoy a good night's sleep free of lice and mice and rats of the human variety.

Fargo waited a while to give the man time to get to his room, then shoved his hands in his pockets, plastered a smile on his face, and ambled inside.

The desk clerk was getting on in years. He had a neatly trimmed speckled beard and speckled hair cut off above the ears, and apparently he was hard of hearing in one ear, because as Fargo approached he tilted his head so his right ear was toward Fargo and loudly declared, "How do you do, friend? If you're after a room, you're in luck. It's late, but we happen to have one handy at the back."

"Thanks, but I don't need one." Fargo was staying in the loft at the stable. He'd had little money on him when he arrived, not dreaming what good fortune awaited him at the poker table.

"Then what can I do for you?"

"I was up a street a ways and thought I saw someone I know come in here," Fargo fibbed. "A drummer I met once. His handle is Smith. Jed Smith."

"Do you mean the fella who just came in about a minute or so ago? A tough customer in a dark suit?"

"That would be him, yes."

"Then he's not your drummer. I have no idea what he does for a living, but his name isn't Smith. It's—" The clerk opened the register and ran a bony finger down the right-hand page. "Ah. Here it is. That was Mr. Colter. Frank Colter. Says here he is out of Washington, D.C."

"How long has he been staying with you?"

The clerk's eyes narrowed. "Since he's not your friend, I don't see where that is any of your concern."

"I'm obliged," Fargo said, and got out of there. The last thing he wanted was for the desk clerk to become suspicious and mention his visit to Colter.

Stymied, Fargo retraced his steps. By now it was close to midnight, but the saloon was packed. Smoke hung thick above the tables. The loud voices, the gruff mirth, the tinkle of chips were as much Fargo's natural element as the wilds. He was halfway to the bar when perfume wreathed him.

"I was beginning to think you had abandoned me," Saucy McBride said in mock sadness.

"Not likely," Fargo said, grinning and wrapping an arm around her slender waist. "What did you have in mind?"

"Why don't I take you to my room and show you?"

4

Saucy McBride's room was above the Hitch Rail. Like most doves, she could ill afford a plush apartment. The room was small and sparse, with a run-down bed, an old table, and two well-worn chairs. Through the thin floorboards wafted the tinny notes of the piano and the hubbub of conversation.

"It's not much," Saucy said apologetically as she stepped aside so he could enter, "but I can't complain. There's a water closet at the end of the hall, and in the winter plenty of heat." She closed the door and threw the latch. "I've stayed at places that were a lot worse."

So had Fargo. Leaning against the table, he commented, "Your boss doesn't mind you bringing men up?"

"My free time is my own to do with as I please." Saucy fluffed her red hair and smoothed her dress. "And before you ask, no, I don't make a habit out of getting acquainted with every gent who strays into the saloon. But now and again a gal needs companionship. Know what I mean?"

Fargo knew all too well. A scout's life was often a lonely one, with days and sometimes weeks spent on the trail, far from human habitation, days and weeks when he did not set eyes on another soul.

"The moment you walked in, I had butterflies in my stomach," Saucy said while opening a cupboard and taking down a whiskey bottle. "You are an uncommonly handsome rascal."

"I'm as ordinary as candle wax."

"Oh, please. I bet you have to beat the ladies off with a club. There isn't a gal alive who wouldn't leap at the chance to bed you."

"I've met a few." Fargo did not care to talk about his escapades with females. Certain things were private.

Saucy produced two glasses, wiped them on a towel hanging from a peg, and set them on a counter. She filled each glass halfway, sipped from hers, and handed the other to him. "It's not the best money can buy, but it's not bad, either." She treated herself to another swallow. "I've long since given up on the notion of ever being rich, so this will have to do."

"You don't hear me complaining." To Fargo, liquor was liquor. He had tasted everything from Georgia moonshine to El Paso tequila, from the finest Scotch to rotgut so watered down it was more water than alcohol.

"You don't say a whole hell of a lot, period," Saucy said, "unless it's to answer me." She drained the rest of her glass at a gulp and poured another. "If you're hungry I have bread and cheese."

"I'm hungry, all right," Fargo said, reaching out and snagging her wrist, "but not for food."

Giggling, Saucy said, "I was beginning to think you were the bashful type. Most men would have ripped my dress off by now."

"Dresses cost money." Pulling her close, Fargo molded his hips to hers. "Or would you rather I don't give a damn?"

"A true gentleman *and* handsome to boot," Saucy marveled. "How is it you're not hitched yet?"

"I've yet to meet a female who doesn't try to talk me to death," Fargo groused. He finished his drink, waited for her to do likewise, and placed both glasses on the table. Then he boldly cupped her bottom with both hands and ground against her. "How about if you kill me with your body instead?"

"Why, sir," Saucy playfully teased, "whatever do you have in mind?"

Fargo covered her lips with his. She responded as if she were famished and he were a feast. Her tongue delved into his mouth and swirled around and around, her bosom swelled against his chest, her thighs molded to his. From deep in her throat came a tiny mew of kindled passion.

When they broke for breath, Saucy was panting. "You sure can kiss," she said, flattering him. "That just about tingled my toes."

"Just about isn't good enough," Fargo said, and kissed her again, harder, his left hand rising along the sweep of her legs to her smooth belly and up over it to cup her right breast. She shivered at the contact, and groaned when he tweaked her nipple through the fabric.

"Keep this up and I'm liable to ravish you," Saucy bantered.

"Promises, promises." Fargo kissed her neck, then fastened his mouth to an earlobe and sucked while he kneaded and caressed her twin melons until they heaved with unleashed desire. Her breath became a furnace, her skin warm to the touch.

"Mmmmmm," Saucy huskily cooed. "That did the trick. My toes will be tingling for a month of Sundays."

"Not long enough." Fargo slid his hands down the backs of her thighs and hoisted her into the air. She took that as her cue to wrap her legs around him and lock her ankles. Her feather-soft lips fluttered to his and her fingers traced the hard outline of his biceps.

Carrying her to the bed, Fargo gently laid her down. Stepping back, he took off his hat and threw it on the table, then peeled off his buckskin shirt.

Saucy's eyes widened. "Oh, my. You have more

muscles than most ten men. A girl could get used to a sight like that."

She jabbered too much, Fargo thought. He silenced her with another kiss that went on and on in languid, molten wetness. His fingers explored every square inch from her knees to her shoulders, and soon he commenced unfastening buttons and undoing stays to get at the charms hidden underneath.

"Oh, yesssss," Saucy breathed, writhing under his erotic ministrations. "You touch me in all the right places."

Fargo leaned over her shoulder and pried with his thumbnail at a tiny button that was being stubborn.

"You would be surprised at how many men don't have any idea what excites a girl." Saucy rambled on. "They treat us like we're a piece of sausage. Or, worse, they can't be bothered to excite us at all so long as they have their fun."

Fargo wished to heaven she would shut up. He was growing impatient with the button and had half a mind to tear the dress off.

"You would think it would come naturally," the chatterbox babbled, "but it has to be learned, like everything else." She chortled. "I thought about opening a school to teach men how to make love but figured I'd be tarred and feathered by the straitlaced crowd for sinning."

The button finally came loose, but there was another under it. Fargo inwardly swore.

"A man told me once, a professor from back east, that in the old days, in a country called Greece, there were ladies who gave lessons in love. His exact words. They taught others how to do it. Can you imagine?"

"Were they any good at sewing mouths shut?"

Saucy's eyebrows pinched together. "How can you kiss someone if your mouth is sewn shut?"

"There's more to kiss than the mouth." Fargo had one button to go, but it resisted his every tug.

"That makes no kind of sense whatsoever," Saucy told him. "What is taking so long? If you don't hurry, you're apt to spoil the mood, and we'll have to start all over."

Growing testy, Fargo sank onto his knees between her legs. If he couldn't shut her up one way, he would do it another. Gripping the hem of her dress, he suddenly peeled the lower half up over her hips and her waist.

"What are you up to down there?"

Fargo's hands were between her legs. It took only a few seconds to part her undergarments. Before she could guess his intent, he fused his lips to her nether mound and slid his tongue along her moist slit.

"Oh, God! Oh, Fargo, yes, yes!" Saucy came up off the bed, arched in a taut bow. Her lips parted and her eyelids fluttered and she hung there as if suspended by invisible wires. Then she cried out and sank back, thrashing her head from side to side.

Fargo applied the tip of his tongue to her swollen knob.

"Like that! Like that! There! There! Oh! What you are doing to me!" Again Saucy launched herself off the bed, and it was a wonder she did not send Fargo flying. Again she collapsed, but this time she clamped her thighs like a vise to his head and entwined her fingers in his hair. "Don't you stop!" she moaned huskily. "Don't you dare by God stop!"

A flick of Fargo's tongue was all it took. Saucy's bottom rose like the prow of a ship in storm-tossed waters. In a frenzy she ground her muff against him while cooing like a lovebird in the throes of delirium. "Harder!" she urged. "Suck me harder! Suck me until I scream!"

Fargo did as she wanted. He did not care that those in adjoining rooms could hear her. He did not care that the customers in the saloon below were probably listening and smirking. He cared only about the satiny feel of her thighs and the sugary nectar that he could never get enough of.

"Fargo! Oh, Fargo!"

Holding on to her hips, Fargo stroked his tongue deep into her womanhood, inciting her to ever higher peaks of arousal. He ran the tip of his tongue across her knob, and she nearly tore his hair out by the roots.

Fargo rose onto his elbows, then on his knees. He undid his belt and his buckskin pants. As he slid them down, her hooded eyes regarded him hungrily.

"Oh, my. I have a stallion on my hands." Saucy grinned. "If I were standing up, I would be weak at the knees." She impishly wrapped her hand around his member and lightly squeezed.

Fargo thought he would explode.

"Like that, do you?" Saucy taunted. She slowly moved her hand up and down, then cupped him below. "Boulders and a redwood. Who would have guessed what was hidden under those britches?" Laughing lightly, she spread her legs wide. "Don't keep me waiting, handsome."

Fargo didn't. He inserted the tip, placed his hands under her backside, and levered up into her the full length of his shaft. Her head snapped back and her mouth opened, but no sound came out. For an instant she froze. Then she buried her fingernails in his shoulders and pulled him down so her bosom cushioned his chest, her nipples like tacks against his skin.

"Ohhhhhh." The moan hung in the air, enveloping them with sound even as Saucy's arms and legs enveloped Fargo in velvet. "You are so hard! I want you! God, how I want you!"

Fargo stroked, almost out, then in. He settled into a rhythm. She matched him, thrust for thrust, tit for tat, her urgency rising as his did. Her cries of wanting mingled with his lustful grunts. Limbs interwoven, they moved faster and faster. The bed under them and the walls around them blurred.

Then came the deluge. Fargo felt Saucy's inner walls contract, and a second later she spurted, drenching his pole. He held his own explosion in, but not for long. All it took was for her to fondle him and he was over the brink. Again and again he drove into her, so hard he thought the bed would break.

Afterward, Saucy's rapid breathing slowed to normal and her lush body stilled. She lay totally spent, beautiful in her nakedness. Fargo placed his cheek on her chest and was lulled by the gentle rise and fall into dozing off. When next he opened his eyes and glanced at the small clock that served as the table's centerpiece, it was almost three in the morning.

Fargo had agreed to meet Arthur Draypool at the hotel at seven. Plenty of time yet. He would catch up on his sleep and start the new day alert and refreshed.

Saucy mumbled in her sleep and smacked her lips. Contentedly nestling her head against his shoulder, she was the portrait of a living angel.

About to doze off again, Fargo could not resist running his fingers through her lustrous red hair.

The crowing of a rooster outside the window woke Fargo up at the crack of daybreak. He dressed swiftly and tiptoed out so as not to awaken Saucy. He had already told her he was leaving, so there would be no hard feelings.

The street was nearly deserted at that early hour. A few neglected horses dozed at the rail in front of the saloon as Fargo bent his steps toward the livery. A cantankerous old cuss brought the Ovaro from its stall while Fargo fetched his saddle, saddle blanket, and bridle from the tack room. Within fifteen minutes Fargo was trotting down the street toward the Sunflower.

Dawn was Fargo's favorite time of the day. The golden crown on the horizon, the brisk chill in the air, the sense of a world astir—all were ripe with the promise of new possibilities. The feeling was similar to that which he experienced whenever he crested a ridge or a pass high in the Rockies and beheld unexplored country.

Arthur Draypool was not waiting outside the hotel as he had promised. Fargo was not surprised. City folk tended to oversleep. He left the Ovaro at the hitch rail and ambled inside, thinking he would go up the stairs to the second floor and pound on Draypool's door. But the clerk had other ideas.

"Mr. Fargo, isn't it? Mr. Draypool left this envelope for you."

It was sealed. Puzzled, Fargo slid a nail along the seam and removed a single sheet of folded paper. The note was short and to the point:

> Mr. Fargo,
> My associates and I will meet you two miles to the northeast on the road to Richmond. We have packhorses and plenty of supplies.
> Yours truly, Arthur Draypool

Fargo thought it odd of Draypool not to mention that his associates, as Draypool kept calling them, were in Kansas City. More of the secrecy that Draypool insisted was necessary to ensure that rumors of the effort to end the Sangamon River Monster's murderous spree did not reach the killer's ears.

To Fargo the precautions seemed more than a trifle silly. They were hundreds of miles from the Monster's haunts. The odds of the killer's learning what Draypool was up to were extremely slim.

Still, Arthur Draypool was paying good money, a lot of good money, and for ten thousand dollars Fargo could put up with a lot of silliness.

What harm could it do?

5

Arthur Draypool was a man of his word. He was waiting for Fargo two miles out of Kansas City on the road to Richmond. The road was not as frequently used as others that linked Kansas City to points east, but Fargo assumed it was more of Draypool's precious secrecy. It did not surprise him that Draypool chose it. What *did* surprise him was the two men with Draypool.

Both spotted Fargo long before he reached them. They were dressed enough alike to be twins: black hats, black frock coats, black pants, and black boots. That was as far as the similarities went. One man stood over six feet, the other barely five. The tall one had curly hair the color of corn and blue eyes. His short companion had straight hair as black as a raven's wing and eyes as dark as pitch.

Spaced well apart, they came to the edge of the road to await him. Neither had a firearm strapped around his waist, but that was deceiving. Barely noticeable bulges under their frock coats revealed where they carried their revolvers. The tall one said something over his shoulder, and Arthur Draypool hurried up to greet Fargo warmly. "Welcome! I was worried you wouldn't find us!"

Fargo had not taken his eyes off the pair in black. His right hand on his Colt, he drew rein in the middle of the dusty road and remarked, "These are the associates you were telling me about?"

"What?" Draypool said, and glanced over his shoulder. "Oh. You must mean the note I left for you. It was, perhaps, an unfortunate choice of words. The associates you are thinking of, the ones I told you about in the saloon, are men of power and prestige in Illinois. Businessmen and politicians who have decided enough lawlessness is enough and want to eliminate the criminals." He gestured at the frock coats. "These two gentlemen work for me and only me. I retain them to safeguard my person from physical harm."

"Do you, now?"

"Permit me to introduce Mr. Bryce Avril," Draypool said, nodding at the tall man with the yellow curls, "and Mr. Vern Zeck." The small man might as well have been carved from marble. "They never do anything separately. Where one goes, the other goes. What one does, the other does. They are reflections of each other, you might say." Draypool grinned crookedly.

"You never mentioned them in Kansas City."

"My apologies," Draypool responded, "but how is that pertinent? They have no bearing on you or our agreement."

Fargo still didn't like it. The pair made his skin itch. The same itch he'd had last month when he spotted a Comanche war party down in Texas, or the month before that when he'd encountered a grizzly in the high country. They were hired killers. Nothing more, nothing less.

Arthur Draypool wasn't a complete fool. "I can send them on ahead if they bother you," he offered.

Avril and Zeck exchanged glances, and the taller man said, "We advise against that, sir. Outlaws infest these Missouri hills. It's not safe."

"Mr. Fargo will protect me," Draypool said. "Both

of you are aware of his reputation. I would be in good hands."

"But not our hands," Zeck said. "Begging your pardon, sir, but he isn't on your payroll. He doesn't give a damn if you live or die."

"And you do?" Fargo broke in.

Avril and Zeck nodded in unison, and the former replied, "We like working for Mr. Draypool. He pays well for our services."

"Extremely well," Zeck amended.

"And we would not take it kindly if anything were to happen to him," Avril warned.

Zeck nodded. "We would not take it well at all."

To Draypool, Avril said, "We will go if you insist, sir, but we will not go far. We will not let you out of our sight."

Vern Zeck nodded. "We will watch over you whether you want us to or not."

"It's up to Mr. Fargo," Draypool said. "I will abide by his decision, whatever it might be."

Fargo had not changed his opinion of the pair. If anything, he distrusted them even more. But it occurred to him that it was better to keep them close so he could keep an eye on them. "They can tag along."

Draypool's relief was transparent. "I thank you, most sincerely. The truth is, I couldn't get by without them. They have been my right and left hands for several years. I rely on them for much more than you can imagine."

"If you say so." Fargo gigged the Ovaro. "Let's head out. It's a long ride to Springfield and I don't aim to be at this all year." He had gone only a hundred yards when hooves clattered and Arthur Draypool brought his mount alongside the pinto and paced it.

"Are you mad at me?"

"Why would I be?" Fargo evaded the question.

"I don't know. But I have the distinct feeling you

are." Draypool waited, and when the seconds stretched on in silence, he coughed and said, "Perhaps we should talk this out. As you noted, we have a long journey ahead, and it won't do to spend it upset. Surely that is reasonable?"

"All I care about is the ten thousand."

"As well you should," Draypool said. "But there is a lot at stake, and it would help matters if we can get along."

"Maybe I'm the wrong man for the job," Fargo said.

"No!" Draypool practically came out of the saddle. "Trust me. No one is more suited. You are just the person we need. A lot of careful planning has gone into this operation."

Fargo could think of half a dozen scouts able to track the Sangamon River Monster, and said so.

"Undoubtedly they could," Draypool said. "But you are the one we want. No one else will suffice."

"Why not?" In Fargo's estimation they were making more of him than he deserved. "Frontiersmen are as common as grass west of the Mississippi."

"But not ones with your talents," Draypool said. "Not ones who have your experience. Not ones whose tracking skills rival an Apache's." He grinned like the proverbial cat that ate the proverbial canary. "You see, I have studied up on you. I have read every newspaper article, every lurid periodical. I know where you were born. I know that if you were in the habit of carving notches on your revolver, you would need a revolver as big as the moon."

"You have me all figured out," Fargo dryly commented.

Draypool giggled. "I flatter myself that I do, yes. When engaging in an enterprise of this nature, it is wise to learn all one can."

"What makes this different from any other manhunt?" Fargo asked.

"The nature of the quarry. You would not hire a

ten-year-old to hunt a bear, would you? By the same token, I would not hire just any simpleton off the street to hunt the Sangamon River Monster." Draypool paused. "Taking him alive will not be easy. I hope you will reconsider your decision not to shoot him on sight."

"I'm not a hired killer." Fargo thought he had made that plain.

"Then you put yourself at a disadvantage, because I can assure you that he will have no compunction about killing you."

"I brought a Mimbres chief in alive once. I can do the same with your renegade," Fargo predicted.

Arthur Draypool frowned and fidgeted. "I appreciate your confidence. I truly do. What will it take to convince you it is misguided?"

"That's a polite way of calling me an idiot," Fargo observed.

"Not at all. I merely don't care to be responsible for your death. It would weigh heavily on my conscience."

Fargo had seen enough buffalo droppings to know when he was hip-deep in the stuff. "We should play poker sometime."

Draypool could not hide his confusion. "I'm sorry. What does that have to do with anything?"

Before Fargo could respond, Bryce Avril trotted up beside them. He was leading their packhorse. There was no sign of Vern Zeck. "We are being followed, sir," he announced.

"You're sure?"

"Yes, sir." Avril twisted and pointed.

At the last bend they had passed, well back from the road and screened by trees so no one coming up the road could see him, sat Zeck astride a bay. Raising an arm, he held up two fingers.

"Perhaps they are innocent travelers," Draypool said.

"Can we afford to take the chance, sir?"

Fargo remembered the man who had followed Draypool the night before, but he did not share the information.

"What would you recommend, Mr. Avril?"

"Fargo and you ride on, sir. Vern and I will catch up after we deal with the two trailing us."

Fargo could have sworn that Draypool quickly glanced at him out of the corner of an eye, as if worried how he would react. But it happened so fast he could not be sure.

"Perhaps we are being hasty, Mr. Avril. After all, this is a public road, open to everyone and sundry. I suggest that Mr. Zeck keep an eye on the two men but not take any action without my express approval."

"Certainly, sir," Bryce Avril said, but he did not sound pleased. Wheeling his mount, he hauled on the lead rope and headed back to tell his partner.

"Shall we?" Draypool showed his teeth. "Please excuse them. They tend to be overzealous on occasion."

Fargo rode on. He had made up his mind what he would do, but he would have to wait until nightfall. "You should send them after the Sangamon River Monster. They wouldn't object to gunning him down."

"If they could track as well as they shoot and ride, I would."

After that Draypool fell silent, for which Fargo was grateful. He never had liked people who were not completely open and honest with him. Draypool was no worse than most, but there was something about him that did not ring true. Fargo could not quite make up his mind what it was.

Fargo tried to tell himself that maybe he was being too mistrustful. He was a loner by nature, always wary of others. To most folks that was unthinkable. They were their own worst company, and were happy only when surrounded by other human beings. Fargo was the opposite. He was happiest when he was by his lonesome. When there were just him and the mountains or the prairie, and no one else. Which was peculiar, given his fondness for saloons and doves. But a man needed his pleasures.

"I had a niece," Arthur Draypool unexpectedly stated.

When the Illinoisan did not go on, Fargo said, "I had a dog once."

"Please. I am baring my soul." Draypool straightened. "Her name was Bethany and she was twelve years old. She was murdered by the Monster. It broke my sister's heart, and she has never been the same." Draypool looked at him. "It's part of why I am so determined to end the madman's reign of terror."

"Your personal life is your own."

"Ordinarily I would agree. But it is important that you understand. That you not take me for a fanatic, or a vigilante."

"What I take you for is the gent who is going to pay me ten thousand dollars," Fargo said.

"It always comes back to the money, doesn't it? Somehow I expected more."

"You're the one who wants the Monster killed," Fargo reminded him.

"Touché. Yes, I do, and yes, that is hardly a proper sentiment, but when a person loses a loved one, proper sentiments fly out the window with mercy and compassion. Revenge is all you think about. Revenge is all you live for."

Fargo could recollect a few such instances in his own life.

"So if I seem too cold and callous, that's why. When Bethany was little I rocked her on my knee. Now she is six feet under, thanks to a beast in human guise. A rabid animal who deserves the fate of all rabid animals." Draypool wagged a finger. "I daresay you would shoot a rabid skunk, or a rabid coyote, or a rabid wolf. Yet you won't bring yourself to shoot him."

The man would not let it drop.

"I'll make up my mind when the time comes to squeeze the trigger." It was the best compromise Fargo could make.

They did not stop at midday. They did not rest at all. Draypool insisted on pushing on until sunset. He wanted to make camp at the side of the road, but Fargo roved among the trees and discovered a clearing where their fire would not be seen by anyone passing by.

Bryce Avril kindled it. He also filled a coffeepot with water from their water skin and put the coffee on to brew. He then left to find Vern Zeck. Twilight had about succumbed to darkness when the underbrush crackled and the two men reappeared. Zeck immediately went to Draypool to report.

"They stopped for the night about half a mile back, sir. If you ask me, they have no intention of overtaking us anytime soon."

Since they did not want a gunshot to give them away, supper consisted of salted beef, potatoes, and bread.

Fargo ate sparingly and washed the food down with two cups of scalding black coffee. Draypool did not say much all evening; he was preoccupied, wrestling with an inner problem. He did instruct Avril and Zeck to take turns keeping watch. Fargo offered to help, but Draypool would not hear of it.

Shortly past ten, Fargo turned in. He was not tired, but he gave the impression he was by yawning a lot and pretending he could not keep his eyes open. He deliberately arranged his blankets near the horses, removed his spurs, and lay on his side facing the fire, with his hat brim pulled low, but not so low that he could not watch the others. Soon Draypool pleaded sleepiness. Since Zeck had the first watch, Avril chose a spot close to their employer and presently was snoring.

Vern Zeck took his job seriously, but he had been up all day, and along about midnight fatigue took its toll. He was feeding bits of a broken branch to the flames, and his chin drooped. Twice he snapped his head up and shook himself. The third time sleep would not be denied.

Slipping from under his blanket, Fargo padded past the horses and on into the woods. He did not have far to go, and he could be much quieter on foot. When he reached the road he turned south and adopted a dogtrot.

Something strange was going on, and it was high time he had some answers.

6

The acrid scent of smoke drew Fargo into the benighted woods on the left side of the road. He had
gone about twenty yards when he spied the red glow
of burning embers and heard a horse nicker. Instantly,
he crouched, then stealthily stalked forward until he
saw two horses in a small clearing. At the center was
the fire, or what was left of it. On either side lay a
huddled figure in a blanket.

It struck Fargo that the pair were not expecting
trouble or one of them would have been standing
guard. Granted, Missouri was not the Rockies, but
there were plenty of outlaws. Their lack of caution
pegged them as greenhorns.

Palming his Colt, Fargo crept nearer. He would give
the pair the benefit of the doubt and treat them as
innocent travelers until they proved otherwise, but he
would be prepared if they were not.

He came to the edge of the trees and hunkered. He
scanned the clearing to ensure there were only the
two. Then he glided toward them, making no more
noise than the breeze. He had several strides left to
take when an ember flared bright for a few seconds,
fanned by a gust, and in its feeble glow something
glinted in the hand of one of the sleepers.

"That's far enough, mister. I am a crack shot and
will kill you where you stand if you do not do exactly
as I say."

Fargo was furious with himself. He had made the sort of stupid mistake he thought they had made.

"Set your pistol on the ground," the man commanded.

Any hopes Fargo entertained of diving flat and snapping off a shot were dashed when the second prone form sat up and coldly declared, "You heard him. Do it and do it fast. My trigger finger is itchy."

Fargo made a mental note to beat his head against a tree at the next opportunity, provided he lived. His lips pressed tight, he tucked at the knees and placed his Colt in front of him.

"Now back up two steps," the first speaker ordered, "and keep your hands where we can see them."

In unison the pair rose. The one on the right immediately circled to the right, the other circled to the left. As soon as Fargo was between them, the man on the left extended his revolver and aimed squarely at Fargo's head. The other man came up and jabbed his revolver into Fargo's ribs.

"What have we here? Don't you know it's not healthy to go sneaking around someone else's camp in the middle of the night?"

"Who are you?" Fargo wanted to know.

The man snorted. "You have this backwards, mister. We're holding guns on you so we get to ask the questions and you supply the answers." He paused. "Who are *you*?"

Fargo debated whether to tell them. It might be wise, he reasoned, to learn more about them first. He used the same name he had given the desk clerk back in Kansas City. "Jed Smith."

"That's strange," said the first man. "There was a trapper and mountain man by that name. The Comanches killed him. Was he a relation of yours?"

"No," Fargo answered. "Now suppose you fess up to who you are and why you are following us."

"Us?" the second man repeated. He was stockier than the other, with a bulbous nose and a jutting chin.

"Cover him," the first man said. "I want a good look at his face." Squatting, he poked a stick in the embers, added kindling, and blew softly on the tiny flames that flared until he had rekindled the fire. "Now then," he said. Rising, he gripped Fargo by the arm and turned him from side to side, studying him.

Fargo repaid the favor and discovered it was the man in the dark suit who had shadowed Draypool back to Draypool's hotel. The one the desk clerk called Frank Colter.

As if in confirmation, the other man asked, "Do you know this tall drink of water, Frank?"

"I can't say as I do, Jim," Colter said. "But I would swear I should. Something about him is familiar."

Jim wagged his revolver. "What is your connection to the League, mister?"

"The what?"

"Don't pretend you don't know," Jim snapped. "By your own admission you are a friend of Arthur Draypool's. That alone is enough to incriminate you."

"I don't know what the hell you are talking about," Fargo said. He was losing his patience, and his temper. He never liked being held at gunpoint.

"Sure you don't," Jim scoffed. "That's why you snuck up on us intending to murder us in our sleep. We're not stupid."

"No, we are not," Frank Colter interjected. "We will go easier on you if you admit the truth. Otherwise, we must take whatever steps we deem necessary."

"I still don't know what you are talking about," Fargo said.

Jim took a half step nearer. "Let me work on him. He won't be so smug after I break a few fingers or bust a few teeth."

Fargo tensed his legs. He would be damned if he would just stand there while they beat on him.

"There will be none of that," Frank Colter said. "Only as a last resort will we do anything drastic."

"As you wish, sir," Jim said with great reluctance. "But you know as well as I do what's at stake. If you ask me, stooping to their level is only fair."

Colter nodded at Fargo. "I'm only offering him a chance to be reasonable. First the carrot, then the stick."

Jim glowered, a keg of powder fit to explode. Shifting his weight from one foot to the other, he thumbed back the hammer of his revolver. "Say the word and I'll start with his legs and work my way up until he confesses. We must find out what they are up to before it is too late."

"What who is up to?" Fargo asked.

"It won't work," Jim scoffed. "Pretend all you want, but we know that you know, and you know that we know you know."

Fargo's patience snapped. "Were you born an idiot or did you have to work at it?" Without warning, Jim swung the revolver at his head. Instinctively, he ducked, but he was not quite quick enough. The barrel clipped him across the temple, not hard enough to knock him out but with sufficient force to drop him to his knees. The world spun chaotically.

"You damned traitor!" Jim snarled, and raised his revolver to do it again.

"Enough!" Frank Colter sprang and seized the other's wrist. "Damn it, Sloane! You will do as I tell you." He held on until Jim Sloane lowered his arm, then said, "I should have brought Pearson along. He knows how to control his temper."

"But the rumors," Sloane said. "The consequences."

"That's no excuse. We will not stoop to their level, as you put it, so long as I am in charge. Do you understand?"

Fargo's head had stopped spinning but was pounding with pain. A moist sensation spread down his cheek. He touched his fingers to his temple. Blood was trickling from a small gash.

"I'm sorry, sir," Sloane apologized to Colter. "I just don't want to see a hundred years count for nothing because—"

A twig snapped loudly in the nearby woods. Fargo glanced up just as a shot boomed and saw the slug catch Jim Sloane high in the right shoulder. The impact jarred Sloane backward. Instantly, Frank Colter spun and fired into the woods, only to be answered with a hail of lead. Colter was hit in the leg, and he, too, staggered, but he did not fall. Suddenly turning, he looped his free arm around Jim Sloane and, limping feverishly, propelled the two of them toward the vegetation. More shots split the night, but they made it to cover.

Fargo saw his Colt on the ground. Shaking his head to clear a few lingering tendrils of dizziness, he scooped it up. Footsteps pounded, and a hand fell on his shoulder.

"Are you all right?" Arthur Draypool asked with legitimate concern. He held a smoking short-barreled Remington. "What in God's name are you doing out here by yourself? What did you hope to accomplish?" He did not wait for an answer but motioned instead to the frock-coated pair who had materialized on either side of him. "After them! They must not escape!"

Like hounds unleashed on fleeing inmates, Avril and Zeck bounded into the forest in pursuit.

"No," Fargo said, slowly rising. His legs would not quite work as they should. Apparently he had been slugged harder than he'd thought. "I want them alive. I want to talk to them."

"They are highwaymen," Draypool said. "They would have killed you had we not come looking for you."

Fargo was willing to wager his last dollar that whatever Colter and Sloane were, they *weren't* common robbers. Colter, in particular, impressed him as someone with a strong sense of honor.

"I couldn't sleep and was tossing and turning," Draypool said. "Then I noticed you were missing. I must say, I was shocked. You should have told us that you were going off alone."

"I don't need nursemaids," Fargo said gruffly. His momentary weakness had passed and he pushed past the Illinoisan, his teeth clenched against the pounding in his head.

"Wait!" Draypool cried, snatching at his sleeve. "Let my men take care of it. That's what I pay them for."

Fargo paid him no heed. He plunged into the woods, paused for only a second to listen, then raced toward the sound of crackling brush. A shot stabbed the dark with flame and smoke. Another answered.

Fargo ran as fast as he dared. He cupped a hand to his mouth to shout for Avril and Zeck not to harm Colter or Sloane, but he did not call out. They wouldn't listen. They answered only to Draypool. To stop them, he must catch up, which proved easier to contemplate than to effect.

More shots were exchanged up ahead. It was impossible to tell who was doing the shooting.

From somewhere behind Fargo, Arthur Draypool shouted for him to wait, adding, "You could hurt yourself stumbling around in the dark!"

Fargo was insulted. He was a frontiersman. He had lived in the wild for more years than Draypool and his hired guns combined.

Another blast rocked the night. On its heels rose an outcry of pain, which was promptly smothered.

Indigo shapes moved a hundred feet away. To avoid being shot by mistake, Fargo halved his speed and bent low. Presently he stopped. The woods were as silent as a cemetery.

"Fargo, please!" Draypool bleated in the distance. "Where are you?"

Fargo warily advanced. Another flurry of man-made thunder caused him to drop flat. It was well he did. Slugs buzzed overhead. One clipped a leaf that gravity zigzagged onto his hand. He glimpsed more movement, but the source was gone before he could identify it.

A minute of quiet passed. Rising partway, Fargo skirted a log. To the east three shots crackled. A thicket barred his way and he angled to the left to go around. A sound stopped him, a low groan bit off short. He crept closer to the thicket and spied a figure sprawled at its base.

Jim Sloane lay on his back, his arms outflung. His hat was missing, his jacket open, revealing dark stains on his shirt. He gave a slight start when Fargo hunkered at his elbow, then blinked and croaked, "You again! Go ahead. Finish me off, you miserable bastard."

Fargo whispered so no one else would hear. "Why were Colter and you following Arthur Draypool?"

"As if you don't know," Sloane spat out. It cost him a fit of coughing that brought flecks of blood to the corners of his mouth.

"If I did I wouldn't ask."

"Let me die in peace, damn you. But remember one thing, mister. You won't win. We won't let you."

Fargo scanned their vicinity but did not spot anyone else. "I said it before, and I'll say it again. I don't know what the hell you are talking about."

Sloane tried to respond but succumbed to more coughing. When he could finally speak, he rasped, "Have your fun. But the government is on to you and the rest of the League. We won't let you light the fuse."

More puzzled than ever, Fargo said, "What League? What fuse? You don't make sense."

Instead of answering, Sloane laughed bitterly, a

laugh nipped by an upwelling of dark rivulets from between his lips. "Damn!" he gurgled. "I'm not long for this world."

"Listen to me," Fargo said. "Draypool has hired me to track down a killer called the Sangamon River Monster. Have you ever heard of him?"

"Now who is not making any sense?" Sloane weakly rejoined. "Who ever heard of a monster in this day and age?"

"It's a man who mutilates and murders whole families," Fargo explained. "In the Sangamon River region near Springfield."

Sloane blanched as pale as a sheet. His eyes swiveled and fixed on Fargo's face. "What did you say?"

Fargo repeated it, elaborating with, "Draypool and some others want to end the bloodshed. That's why they hired me."

"Oh, God."

"What?" Fargo asked, unsure of whether the man was agitated by the information or had gone stark pale due to his wounds.

"Those devils! It's so simple!" Quaking violently, Sloane raised his head and feebly clawed at Fargo's leg. "He has to be warned! Get word to—"

"To who?" Fargo prompted.

Jim Sloane went rigid. Tears streamed from his eyes as his mouth worked soundlessly. Abruptly going limp, he slumped onto his back and exhaled.

Fargo felt for a pulse but there was none. He heard Draypool huff and puff up behind him, but he did not turn.

"Is that one dead?"

"Yes."

"Good riddance. Let's hope Avril and Zeck do the same with the other."

7

Fargo said very little to Arthur Draypool over the next several days. He did not tell Draypool what Sloane had told him. Better he kept the information to himself until he found out what was going on.

Avril and Zeck had seen to Sloane's burial after they returned from chasing Frank Colter. Colter got away, which secretly pleased Fargo. He offered to help dig Sloane's grave but Draypool would not hear of it. "Menial chores are why I have Mr. Avril and Mr. Zeck in my employ."

As the pair in frock coats busied themselves with broken branches, scooping out earth, Fargo searched Sloane's pockets. He hoped to find something that would tell him who Sloane had been and what Sloane and Colter were up to, but all he found was thirty dollars, a folding knife, and a compass.

In an effort to justify the shooting, Arthur Draypool had gone on and on about the dangers of traveling in that part of Missouri. "Scoundrels are everywhere. It shouldn't surprise you that two of them were following us. No doubt at the first opportunity they planned to relieve us of our valuables, if not our lives."

That was three nights ago. Over the subsequent days, Fargo racked his brain for an excuse to bow out. All he had to do was walk up to Draypool and flatly refuse to go another mile. But he could not bring himself to do it. Part of the reason was that he had agreed to do the job, and while his promise was not carved in granite, he never went back on his word if he could help it.

Curiosity was also a factor. Colter and Sloane had given the impression that Draypool was up to no good. The idea seemed preposterous. Fargo could not for the life of him figure out what Draypool hoped to gain by deceiving him. Why go to so much trouble to track him down and offer him so much money if the whole arrangement was underhanded?

For the time being Fargo was content to go along. But he was no man's fool, and he stayed alert for gleanings of Draypool's true intentions.

The day came when they crossed the border into Illinois. Fargo reckoned they would push on to the next town and rest there for the night. But to his surprise, after only a few miles, Arthur Draypool turned off the main road and down a long lane that brought them to a stately farmhouse. It reminded Fargo of mansions he had seen in the deep South. Scores of workers, nearly all of them black, were busy at various tasks.

"I hope you won't mind if we stop early tonight," Draypool commented. "I thought it might do to treat you to some Illinois hospitality."

Apparently word of their coming had preceded them, for four people were waiting on a broad porch. For farmers, the four were dressed in remarkably nice clothes. A craggy-faced man with a bushy mustache came down the steps to greet them, declaring, "Arthur! What a pleasure to see you again!"

"Permit me to introduce Clyde Mayfair," Draypool said while shaking their host's hand. "He and I go back a long ways."

"I should say so!" Mayfair exclaimed. "We grew up in South Carolina not twenty miles from one another." He went to say more, seemed to change his mind, and instead gestured at the trio coming down the steps behind him. "This is my wife, Margaret, my son, Jace, and my daughter, Priscilla."

"How do you do, sir?" the wife said. Her hair was graying and she had a plump body that jiggled when she moved.

"A pleasure, sir." Jace gave a courtly bow. He was in his twenties, and the spitting image of his sire.

Fargo was more interested in the daughter. Tall and willowy, Priscilla Mayfair filled out her dress in the shape of an hourglass—a rather tight dress for a farm girl, cut low in front to accent her cleavage and snug at the thighs to accent something else. She offered her hand with a graceful flourish.

"I do declare. Aren't you a handsome devil!"

Grinning, Fargo imitated the son's bow and kissed the back of her hand. Only she was aware that he pressed the tip of his tongue to her skin. "I'm pleased to make your acquaintance."

"Not half as pleased as I am," Priscilla said, her lovely green eyes twinkling. She did not resent the liberty he had taken. Quite the contrary.

"Why don't we all go inside?" Clyde Mayfair proposed. "I will have refreshments brought."

Fargo shucked his Henry from the saddle scabbard, untied his saddlebags, and followed Draypool and their hosts indoors.

A butler and two maids, all of them black, snapped to attention as if they were soldiers on a parade ground. Clyde Mayfair had one of the maids take Fargo's personal effects upstairs. Then he said, "Follow me, gentlemen," and led the way to a sitting room.

The house was a model of elegance. Mayfair was no simple farmer. He had money, lots of it, and he was lavish in spending it. Fargo found himself in a plush chair across from a giant window that afforded a sweeping vista of the thousands of acres Mayfair owned. The butler brought him a cup of coffee on a sterling silver tray. The cup itself was of the best china.

Draypool sank into another chair with a contented sigh. The maid gave him a glass of brandy, which he sniffed, then sipped, savoring it as if it was liquid gold. "You have no idea, Clyde, how wonderful it is to be back among civilized society."

"Had a rough time, did you, Arthur?" Margaret Mayfair asked.

"You have no idea. I cannot describe it in mixed company," Draypool assured her. "Suffice it to say that everything you have heard about the frontier is true. It is overrun with barbarians who have no appreciation for the niceties of life."

Fargo almost laughed. If Draypool thought Kansas City was wild and woolly, he should visit a few prairie towns or some of the mining camps up in the Rockies. Compared to them, Kansas City was as tame as Paris or London.

"How sad." Margaret Mayfair sniffed. "People these days have lost all sense of decorum. It comes from bad breeding."

Clyde glanced sharply at Fargo, then cleared his throat and said, "Yes, my dear. I wholeheartedly agree. But we don't want to bore our guest with a discussion about the decline and fall of American culture."

"It would bore me," Priscilla remarked, drawing a barbed look from her mother. "We hear it nearly every day."

"That will be quite enough, young lady," Margaret chided. "When I was your age I would never have presumed to be so impertinent."

"When you were my age," Priscilla said sweetly, "you were as straitlaced as your corset, Mother, and nothing has changed."

Clyde flushed and started to rise, but caught himself. "That will be enough, young lady. Must you constantly bait your mother and I over trifles?"

"My apologies, Father," Priscilla said with mock

sincerity. "I meant no disrespect. But we *have* talked about it endlessly, and it *does* so bore me."

Bestowing an embarrassed smile on Fargo, Clyde said, "Please excuse my daughter's antics. We spoiled her growing up, I'm afraid, and her maturity has suffered as a result."

Now it was Priscilla who colored and clenched her small hands into fists. "There you go again. Carping on my presumed flaws. But I do not have to sit here and listen." She began to rise.

"Sit back down!" Clyde's command had the same effect as the crack of a bullwhip; his daughter flinched, and did as she was told.

Arthur Draypool was nervously running his hands along the polished arms of his chair. "Perhaps we have come at an awkward time and should take our leave."

"Nonsense," Clyde said. "Parents must keep their offspring in line. I am sure our other guest does not think less of us."

All eyes swung to Fargo. "I will if I don't get a glass of whiskey," he said good-naturedly.

"You would rather have that than coffee? How remiss of me." Clyde snapped his fingers and the butler scampered to comply.

Jace Mayfair had not said a word the whole time. He had been studying Fargo, and now he shifted toward him, crossed his legs, and remarked, "I have heard you are one of the best trackers alive."

Since no one had mentioned anything about Fargo's profession since they had arrived, he responded, "Who told you that?"

"Mr. Draypool, before he left."

Arthur smiled and spread his hands. "Clyde is one of my oldest and dearest friends. He believes, like I do, that we must take steps to clean up our fair state. In fact, he put up a portion of the ten thousand dollars."

Clyde Mayfair nodded. "When the law can't do

what it is supposed to do, decent men must take the law into their own hands. I frown on vigilantism, but it can't be helped. Our group is devoted to the greater public good."

"How many of you are there?" Fargo inquired.

"Oh, about a dozen so far," Clyde said vaguely. "But more will rally to our cause before too long. Wait and see."

"Ours is a great and holy crusade," Margaret commented. "We will not rest until Illinois is exactly like the sovereign and law-abiding state of South Carolina."

Jace had not taken his eyes off Fargo. "I like to hunt, and I have done some tracking, but I am an amateur compared to men like you and Hiram Trask."

"Who?"

"Trask is from down South," Jace explained. "He lives deep in the backwoods. He's not as famous as you, but he can track anything that lives, anywhere, anytime. Maybe you will run into him someday."

"You never know," Fargo said.

Jace's mouth quirked upward. "It would be interesting to have a contest between the two of you to determine who is the king of the trackers, as it were."

Clyde Mayfair made what Fargo took to be an impatient gesture. "Don't be silly, son. Trask operates out of Georgia, and it is unlikely Mr. Fargo will venture south of the Mason-Dixon Line anytime soon. His usual haunts are much farther west. Isn't that right?"

Fargo acknowledged that it was.

"Still, it would be interesting," Jace insisted with that enigmatic grin. "It isn't often that men of their caliber are pitted against one another."

"Let's change the subject," Arthur proposed, and he began asking Mayfair questions about the state of the farm, the state of Mayfair's crops, and the weather.

Now it was Fargo who was bored. He gulped the whiskey the butler brought and nursed a second. With nothing better to do, he admired Priscilla Mayfair's tantalizing figure. She met his scrutiny with amused interest, undressing him with her eyes. When she thought no one else was looking, she grinned and winked.

The night ahead promised to be entertaining. Fargo looked forward to getting to know Priscilla a lot better. But first he had to endure another half hour of idle chatter. Then Clyde Mayfair took it into his head to give him a tour of the grounds.

"Something to do until supper."

Once they were outside, Margaret wanted to show Fargo her flower gardens, which she claimed were the grandest in Illinois. At one point she pointed at a rose and said, "Have you ever seen one so big?"

Priscilla bent down and sniffed. "I like the big ones," she said casually, and when she unfurled, she peeked at Fargo from under her long lashes to see if he got the point.

Talking animatedly about his breeding stock, Clyde steered Fargo to the stable. "Thoroughbreds, all of them," he boasted of the twenty horses in their twenty stalls. "Some I've obtained from as far away as England."

"Where is that new stallion you wrote me about?" Arthur Draypool asked, and everyone drifted toward a stall at the end.

Not Fargo. He hung back, and so did Priscilla. She was patting a mare. He moved over next to her. "Don't you like stallions as much as you do big ones?"

An unladylike snort burst from Priscilla's throat and she covered her mouth to smother it. "My, my, aren't you naughty?"

"You're one to talk." Fargo lowered his voice. "When and where?"

"Why, sir, I have no idea what you mean," Priscilla responded with a blank expression.

"I don't play games, girl."

Priscilla glanced at the others, then whispered without looking at him, "Neither do I. But I must be careful. If my parents find out, my father will have you shot."

"When and where?" Fargo repeated.

Jace was strolling back toward them.

"Ten o'clock," Priscilla whispered. "Under the maple east of the stable. For God's sake, don't let anyone see you sneaking out." Straightening, she said loud enough to be heard, "I ride every day, rain or shine. If you were staying longer, I would show you a wonderful spot for a picnic."

"Knowing you, that isn't all you would show him, dear sister," Jace lewdly declared.

"Don't be crude," Priscilla scolded.

"Come now," Jace said. "You're the one who has been making cow eyes at him, not me."

"I mean it," Priscilla said.

Chuckling, Jace nudged her. "You can pull the wool over Mother's and Father's eyes, but never mine. You would do well to remember that."

"And you would do well to remember that I know about your visits to a certain shack out by the cornfields. Father would disown you if he ever discovered you are cavorting with a darky."

Jace seized her wrist. "Don't you ever threaten me, you hear?"

"Oh, please," Priscilla said in contempt, and pulled free. "We each have our secrets, brother mine, and neither of us will betray the other." She smiled at Fargo and walked off, her hips swinging invitingly.

"Damn her!" Jace grumbled. "Damn all women. We should lock them in chains and keep them at the foot of our beds, like dogs." He glanced at Fargo. "What do you think?"

"I think I need another whiskey."

8

She was late.

Fargo had snuck out of the house shortly before ten and had been waiting at the maple tree for almost half an hour. Priscilla had yet to appear. He began to wonder if she had changed her mind, or if something had come up to prevent her from keeping their tryst. He hoped not. He was looking forward to treating himself to her charms.

The farm lay quiet under the stars. The field hands had long since retired to their shacks, marked by tiny squares of light in the near distance. The wide stable doors were shut and barred for the night, the chicken coop closed, the hogs and sheep in their pens. In a pasture beyond the stable cows dozed.

The air had cooled with the setting of the sun, but it was too muggy for Fargo's liking. He preferred the dry air of the mountains and the desert to the humid East.

From inside the great house music wafted. Margaret was playing the piano. She had treated Fargo and Draypool to a recital after supper, and it had been all Fargo could do to stay awake.

Shifting, Fargo leaned against the trunk. He would wait five more minutes. If Priscilla did not show by then, he would turn in. He could do with a good night's sleep in a soft bed.

Off in the woods an owl hooted. A cow lowed as if

in answer. In the stable a horse whinnied. Ordinary sounds in an ordinary night in southern Illinois.

Fargo sighed and shifted his weight, and spotted Priscilla, framed in a ground-floor window. She was beckoning him. Amused by her antics, Fargo hooked his thumbs in his gun belt and ambled to the back door. She opened it just as he reached it, grabbed his arm, and practically yanked him off his feet pulling him inside.

"Thanks for keeping me waiting."

Priscilla put a finger to her lips and ushered him into a small sewing room. She shut the door and whispered, "Don't blame me! I was on my way out when I saw him."

"Who?" Fargo found it hard to concentrate with her warm, lush body so tantalizingly close.

"The one who has been spying on you. He's over by the shed where we store the plow and the harrow."

An icy chill that had nothing to do with the temperature rippled down Fargo's spine. "Describe him."

"I can do better than that. It's Bryce Avril, one of Arthur's bodyguards."

"Is he still out there?"

"I think so. I saw him run from the far corner of the house to the shed, and he never reappeared. I imagine he has been there the whole time, watching you."

"Wait here," Fargo said, and opened the door a crack.

Priscilla brushed against him, her hand rising to his shoulder. "What are you going to do?"

"I don't like being spied on." Simmering with anger, Fargo bent and began removing his spurs. Avril had to be acting under Draypool's orders. No doubt they had been keeping an eye on him the entire time, which begged the question, Why? Was Draypool afraid he would change his mind and leave? Or was there more involved? He would sneak out a window and circle around to the shed. "Here." He handed his right spur to Priscilla.

"I've always wanted to wear a pair of these. But I thought the kind they use out west have bigger rowels."

"Some do," Fargo confirmed, "but they're more for show than anything else. A good rider doesn't need to rip his horse to ribbons to get it to go."

"Oh, I would never do that to a poor animal," Priscilla said. "I like the rowels because they are shiny and bright."

"The big rowels," Fargo teased. "Don't forget you like them big."

Priscilla giggled and jangled the spur. "You are worse than naughty! You are deliciously wicked! I am sick to death of the stodgy sorts I must put up with around here day in and day out."

"A girl your age?" Fargo had the other spur off and held it out to her.

"Before young gentlemen can call on me, they must pass my mother's muster," Priscilla explained. "And my mother's standards are not the same as mine. They are the complete opposite, in fact."

"Whoever courts you must keep their hands off," Fargo guessed.

"Whoever courts me must not even think of touching me because if Mother catches us, I will never see him again," Priscilla lamented. She brightened and raised a finger to his cheek. "You have a lot of missed opportunities to make up for."

Fargo was about to say he was glad to oblige when they both heard the sound of the back door opening. Covering her mouth with his left hand, he peered out. None other than Bryce Avril had just slipped inside. Fargo guided Priscilla to one side and whispered, "Don't move."

Avril came down the hall as if treading on eggshells. He was staring toward the far end, evidently wary of being caught.

Fargo let him go past the sewing room, then silently opened the door and stepped to the middle of the hall. "Looking for someone?"

Avril nearly jumped out of his shoes. Whirling, he streaked his right hand under his jacket. "You!" he blurted. "You shouldn't sneak up on people like that. You're liable to get yourself shot."

"And you shouldn't spy on people who don't care to be spied on," Fargo said. "You're liable to get yourself hurt." And with that, he slugged Avril in the gut. He did not use all his strength, but the blow still doubled the man over and left him sputtering and clutching the wall for support. "Tell your boss that if I ever catch you spying on me again, I won't be nearly as nice about it."

A scarlet tinge spread from Avril's neck to his hairline. He coiled, with his right hand clawed to draw. "You son of a bitch! No one does that to me!"

"Try," Fargo said softly, his own hand next to his holster.

Something in his tone caused Avril to hesitate. "You had no call to hit me. I was only doing my job. Zeck and me are supposed to take turns watching you."

"Not anymore," Fargo said.

"But Mr. Draypool was quite specific," Avril disclosed. "We're not to let you out of our sight. He's worried something might happen to you."

"Tell Draypool," Fargo said, still speaking softly, "that if I catch Zeck or you anywhere near me, something will happen to him." Indulging in threats was childish, but in this instance Fargo could not resist.

"Mr. Draypool won't like this. He won't like it one bit."

"You must have me confused with someone who

gives a damn," Fargo responded. He wagged his fingers. "Off you go."

Simmering with resentment, Avril backed away. "All right. I'll do as you want. But if Mr. Draypool orders us to watch you anyway, that's exactly what we'll do, mister."

Fargo did not move until the man in the frock coat had disappeared around the far corner. Then he slipped into the sewing room, closed the door, and turned, nearly colliding with Priscilla.

"You were magnificent."

"I was mad."

"No, really," Priscilla gushed breathlessly. "You put him in his place. He was scared of you. I could see it on his face."

Fargo put his hands on her hips. "Now that he's gone, we can make up for those missed opportunities of yours."

"Here?" Priscilla said in disbelief. "It's safer outdoors. I know plenty of places where we can be alone and no one will find us."

"Does anyone ever use this room at night?" Fargo asked, and kissed her lightly on the neck.

"Not this late," Priscilla admitted. "But it's insane! It's too dangerous! It could get me in more trouble than I have ever been in." She paused, and her luscious lips formed a sensual invitation. "What are we waiting for?"

Fargo fused his mouth to hers and was unprepared for her reaction. A low moan issued from the depths of her being and she flung her arms and one leg around him and clasped him to her as if she were trying to climb inside his skin. Her tongue darted into his mouth and met his in satiny swirls. He felt her fingernails dig into his arms and back.

Fargo's hands roved over her hips and her flat belly to the swelling curves of her breasts. He covered them, and Priscilla shivered as if she were cold, when actually her body temperature seemed to jump ten degrees. Her nipples were like tacks straining to pierce her dress. He pinched one and then the other and then both at the same time, eliciting whimpers of joy.

"You do things to me no man ever has," Priscilla whispered huskily when she broke for breath.

Fargo doubted that. He ran the tip of his tongue along her chin to her neck and fastened his lips to an earlobe. She sighed and arched her back.

"I'm sensitive there."

In Fargo's estimation she was sensitive everywhere. But he lingered, sucking on the lobe and rimming her ear with his tongue. Her knee rose between his legs, sliding up his inner thighs, causing his manhood to become as hard as iron and to bulge against his buckskin pants. She rubbed her knee over him.

"Mmmmm," Priscilla breathed. "I was right about you. This will be a night to remember."

Fargo hoped she wasn't a chatterbox. To forestall her from talking, he planted another hungry kiss on her wet mouth and kept his mouth there while his hands caressed and kneaded and molded her upper body as if she were clay and he a master sculptor.

Priscilla could not stand still. She squirmed, she wriggled, she wrapped a leg around him and unwrapped it and wrapped it around him again. Her hands roamed everywhere she could reach, from the crown of his head to below his belt. She gasped when she touched him down there.

"You *are* a stallion!"

Pressing her against the wall, Fargo hiked her dress up.

"Standing up?" Priscilla said. "I love it! I just love it! Do with me what you will."

Fargo intended to. Once again he covered her mouth with his. He had her dress midway up her legs, and it only took a few seconds to loosen the last obstacle and for his fingers to find her core. She was moist for him. At the contact, she rose up onto the tips of her toes and exhaled all the breath in her lungs.

"Ohhhhhhhh!"

Her cotton drawers slid down around her knees. Fargo glided his finger along her slit, and when he touched her knob, she threw her head back and bit her lower lip to stifle a carnal outcry. He slowly inserted his finger, immersing it in molten lava, and felt her inner walls ripple.

"Yes! Do me! I can't wait!"

She would have to. Fargo was not quite ready. He added a second finger. Her sheath clung to them, sparking a deluge of hot, hungry kisses lavished on his face and throat.

Fargo commenced pumping his fingers, over and over, slightly faster as he went. Priscilla ground against his hand, her thighs clamped tight to imprison it. But that did not stop him from stroking on and on until she abruptly sank her teeth into his shoulder and moaned. She came, her bottom bucking wildly, threatening to snap his hand from his wrist. He waited, and when she subsided, temporarily spent, he slid his fingers out and brought both hands up to her bosom. He had not yet freed her breasts, but now he remedied that oversight and was rewarded when her glorious globes inflated to twice their previous size. Her nipples were irresistible. He inhaled one, switched to the other, then back again.

"I want you," Priscilla breathed. "I want you inside of me."

Her fingers enfolded Fargo's member. She guided him between her legs, raised her chemise higher, and had him where she desired him. Eagerly, she ran his dripping knob across her nether lips. Then, rising up, she fed his pole into her, inch by inch by inch. She made no sound until he was all the way in. Then she leaned back, closed her eyes, and groaned.

To Fargo's amazement, tears formed. "Are you all right?"

"I am in heaven," Priscilla cooed. "I could do this

every hour of every day." She looked at him. "You don't know how good this feels. You don't know what it's like, being denied for so long. I would shoot my mother if I didn't love her so much."

In one respect she was wrong; Fargo *did* know how good it felt. He held himself still, letting her savor the moment.

"I wish—" Priscilla began, and suddenly stopped and stiffened. "Did you hear something?"

Fargo shook his head.

"Are you sure?" Priscilla whispered. "I thought I heard a footstep out in the hall. Maybe Avril came back."

Fargo leaned as far toward the door as he could, but it was not quite far enough. "Wrap your legs around me," he directed, and when she had complied, he slid along the wall and peeked out. A maid was moving down the hall away from them.

"What if she heard us?" Priscilla asked, aghast.

"Unlikely," Fargo said.

They watched until the maid was gone. The woman did not glance back or in any way betray that she knew they were there.

"Thank goodness!" Priscilla said. "Now where were we?"

Fargo eased the door shut and braced both legs. He gripped her hips, tucked at the knees, and thrust, the first of many. He did not count them, so he could not say if it was the fortieth or the sixty-first when Priscilla bucked in a wanton frenzy of release. His own explosion was not long after.

Breathless, they sagged against one another. Eventually Fargo stirred and began to peel himself from her.

"What do you think you're doing, handsome?" Priscilla asked, wearing an impish expression. "That was only the main course. I haven't had dessert yet. Are you up for it?"

Was he ever.

9

Much to Fargo's annoyance, they did not leave the Mayfair farm until ten the next morning. He was up before daybreak, as was his habit, and ready to head out as a golden crown blazed the eastern sky. But Arthur Draypool wanted to have breakfast with their hosts, and breakfast for the Mayfairs was an affair almost as elaborate as supper. The family gathered around the big table and were waited on by the servants. The fare was worthy of a restaurant: coffee, tea, milk, or juice; ham, bacon, beef, or venison; eggs, flapjacks, johnnycakes, and cracklin' bread.

Fargo had no intention of eating a big meal, but once he sipped some orange juice and nibbled at a johnnycake, his stomach imitated an earthquake, prompting him to heap food high on his plate. He blamed Priscilla. She had been insatiable. They had stayed in the sewing room until nearly two in the morning.

Now she sat across from him, as demure and prim and proper as a true lady was expected to be. She would glance at him every now and then, when she thought no one else was looking, and smile a quick secret smile that only the two of them understood.

Toward the end of the feast, after Fargo had pushed his plate back and patted his overfull stomach, Clyde Mayfair tapped a glass with a spoon to get everyone's attention and declared, "We wish you all the best in your hunt for the Sangamon River Monster, Mr. Fargo. It is a dangerous enterprise, and I trust you will not take it lightly."

"I never take killers lightly," Fargo said.

"You must be diligent in the hunt, merciless when you catch him," Mayfair went on. "If you find your resolve waning, just think of all the poor people that fiend has murdered."

The man had gall, lecturing him, Fargo reflected. He nodded and responded, "I know my job."

Mayfair glanced at Draypool, then said, "I am certain you do. Yet Arthur tells me that you refuse to shoot the Monster on sight."

"I made it plain I don't kill for money. If that's what he wants done, he should have hired someone else."

"Please don't be offended," Clyde said. "Trackers of your caliber are as rare as hen's teeth."

"What about that Hiram Trask your son told me about?" Fargo asked.

It was Draypool who answered. "Trask never leaves the South, where he grew up. He is active mainly in Georgia, Alabama, and Florida."

"A true son of the South," Jace Mayfair remarked.

Both Draypool and Jace's father looked at him sharply, and Clyde Mayfair said, "In these trying times, one should not make such distinctions. They might be misunderstood."

"What does he care?" Jace said testily, and bobbed his chin at Fargo. "How do you feel, exactly, about the coming conflict?"

"I haven't thought about it much," Fargo admitted. He tended to fight shy of politics. "But I don't like the notion of one man owning another."

"Slavery has been around for thousands of years," Jace said. "It's not as if the South invented it. Hell, there are Yankees who own slaves."

Clyde Mayfair smacked the table hard. "I will thank you not to use such language in the presence of your

78

mother and sister. As for slavery, it is hardly a fit topic for our morning meal."

"I just wanted to know where he stood." Jace was in a contrary mood. "Before long, Father, everyone will have to decide where they stand, whether they want to or not."

Clyde smiled at Fargo. "You must excuse him. He's young, and the young are always too headstrong for their own good."

Priscilla set down her orange juice. "Why pick on Jace?" she said, coming to her brother's defense. "You've said the same things he just did many a time."

"I repeat," Clyde Mayfair sternly declared. "Slavery is not a fit topic for polite conversation."

Fargo thought Mayfair was making a fuss over nothing, but he did not say anything, and the family finished the meal in strained silence. Draypool sent Avril and Zeck to bring the horses around, and refilled his teacup one last time.

"It will be a while before we eat this grand again," Draypool said. "Please indulge me, Mr. Fargo, for a few minutes more."

Fargo shrugged.

Clyde leaned his elbows on the table, then took them off at a disapproving stare from his wife. "Tell me about the Indians out your way. I am most curious. From all we hear, they are veritable savages, are they not?"

"Indians are people like us," Fargo said, and added, without consciously meaning to, "The same as blacks or any others."

Clyde reddened. "I beg to differ, sir. Indians are not just like us. They wear animal hides and live in squalor."

"I wear animal hides," Fargo said, touching his buckskin shirt, "and most nights I sleep on the ground wrapped in a blanket."

"You didn't sleep on the ground last night. Look around you, sir. You are seated in a sterling example of why we are superior in every way to every other race."

Fargo decided he disliked Clyde Mayfair. He disliked him a lot. "Indians couldn't pack up and move a house like this, and they move often, to be near buffalo and for other reasons."

"You equivocate, sir. I am not an imbecile. Not all Indians follow the herds. Some live in villages year-round. Villages, need I remind you, ridden with filth and lice and barely fit for human habitation."

"That's enough," Draypool said.

"I am only trying to make a point," Clyde said to justify himself. "We are *not* like the Indians and never will be."

Fargo had listened to enough. He pushed his chair back and stood. "I'll wait with the horses." As he crossed the room to where he had deposited his saddlebags and rifle, Draypool gave an angry hiss.

"That was a mistake, Clyde. You should know better. Need I remind you of the trouble we have gone to, or what's at stake?"

"Don't lecture me."

Fargo was spared the rest of their petty bickering. He strode down the front hall and out into the morning sun and blinked in the bright glare. Another muggy day was in store.

The Ovaro was saddled and waiting. Fargo slid the Henry into the scabbard and secured the saddlebags. The saddle creaked as he forked leather. An urge came over him to say to hell with the whole thing and head for the Rockies, but he stayed where he was, and shortly Draypool and the Mayfairs trickled out, the two men still squabbling.

". . . is that we have to stand up for our own kind," Clyde was saying. "It is our obligation, if you will."

"There is a time and a place for everything," Arthur said, "and this was neither."

A servant held out the reins to his mount and Arthur took them and climbed stiffly on without so much as a thank-you.

Margaret came down the steps and smiled up at Fargo. "Men and their silly spats. Yet they constantly poke fun at us women."

Priscilla sashayed to her mother's side. "If you are ever back this way, be sure to stop by. You are always welcome to our hospitality."

Her hidden meaning brought a grin to Fargo's face. "I'll keep that in mind," he said.

Arthur raised an arm as if it were a lance and exclaimed, "Onward with our quest, gentlemen!"

All that day they traveled hard. Draypool had a new urgency about him, which was puzzling to Fargo in light of their leisurely stay at the Mayfair farm. They left the main road and traveled to the northeast along byways and back ways that only someone completely familiar with the region would know. Zeck was that someone; he assumed the lead about noon. Toward evening, when Fargo asked how it was that Zeck knew every rutted track and path, the small man in black mentioned that he had grown up in the area.

And what an area it was! Fargo had seldom seen such lush woodland, verdant forest abundant with vegetation and wildlife, not at all like the arid timberland of the Rockies. For one thing, there were more leafy trees than pines, more maples and elms and willows and oaks than firs or spruces. For another, the undergrowth was a jungle compared to the sparse brush of the mountains. Green, green, everywhere, a profusion born of rich soil and that most precious of all nature's gifts, water. The annual rainfall was many times that received by the land west of the Mississippi, creating countless waterways.

One of the largest in central Illinois was the Sanga-mon River. Draypool remarked to Fargo that the river flowed over two hundred and fifty miles. Rising in Champaign County, it eventually merged with the Illinois River, which, in turn, fed into the mighty Mississippi.

Draypool had been right about the extent of Illinois wilderness. Somehow Fargo had gotten it into his head that the state was all farmland and towns and cities, but such was not the case. The southern third was largely settled, and more and more people flocked to the north end of the state, and Chicago, every year. But the rest was pristine woodland, as wild and un-tamed as anything on the frontier.

Wildlife was everywhere. All kinds of birds, from tiny wrens and chickadees to catbirds and red-breasted robins to hungry hawks and turkey vultures. All kinds of small animals, from squirrels and raccoons and opossums to muskrats and even beavers. Predators, too, in the form of foxes and cougars and black bears.

That night they camped in the woods by a small stream. Avril shot a rabbit for supper and roasted it on a spit.

Draypool had been edgy all day, and now, as they were eating, he glanced at Fargo and said, "From here on out we must exercise extreme care. No one must learn what we are up to."

Biting into a rabbit leg, Fargo chewed the juicy meat with relish.

"Did you hear me?"

"I'm sitting three feet from you," Fargo said with his mouth full.

"Secrecy is of the utmost importance. We don't want word to get back to the devil we are after."

"Who in their right mind would warn him?" Fargo asked. "After all he's done?"

"You know how gossip and rumors spread," Draypool said. "And remember, we have no idea who the Sangamon River Monster is. It could be anyone."

"Which reminds me," Fargo said. "How am I to track him? Do we wait around for him to strike and I pick up his trail?"

"That is one option, yes. But the group I work with has been quietly trying to learn his identity. We have a network of informers at our disposal. And we have a description to go by. The Monster is a man in his forties, maybe early fifties. He is tall, over six feet, and rather thin. He has a beard but no mustache."

"That could fit hundreds of men," Fargo noted.

"True. But we also know he has black hair, a big nose, and big ears. That narrows it down some."

Still, it was like looking for a needle in a giant haystack, and Fargo said so.

"Does that mean we give up before we begin?" Draypool responded. "I should say not! Think of all those this man has killed. Think of those he will slay in the future if he is not stopped."

"I didn't say I wouldn't do it."

"We are counting on you," Draypool said. "More than you can imagine. The success or failure of our enterprise rests entirely on your shoulders. Are you up to the challenge? Have I made a mistake?"

"I'll do what I can." Fargo would not make promises he could not keep.

Draypool gave him a searching scrutiny and sighed. "We can only hope for the best. We will help you every step of the way as best we are able."

Later, Fargo lay on his back under his blanket, his arm pillowing his head, and gazed absently up at the sparkling myriad of stars. He felt uneasy, and he could not say why, which added to his unease. It wasn't the risk he was taking in going after a butcher like the Monster. He had tangled with the likes of the Apaches and the Comanches, and certain white outlaws and badmen who were every bit as formidable. No, it was something else. But what? He racked his brain for over an hour. He reviewed all that had happened since he met Draypool. And when he was done, the unease still gnawed at him, and he still could not say why. Then sleep claimed him.

The next day was a repeat of the previous one. Zeck stuck to the less-used roads. Whenever they came upon other travelers, Draypool visibly tensed and came up close to Fargo. Yet another puzzlement.

At midday they stopped at the side of the road. The packs on one of the packhorses were loose, and Draypool instructed Avril and Zeck to tighten them. Dismounting, Draypool sat in the shade of a maple and dabbed at his perspiring brow with a handkerchief.

"I have never gotten used to this damnable humidity."

"I need to stretch my legs." Fargo pushed his hat back on his head and strolled into the woods.

"Don't be gone long," Draypool called after him. "We have many miles to travel yet today."

A gray squirrel chattered at Fargo from high in a tree. Sparrows chirped and frolicked. Crows were active to the west, their *caw-caw-caw* borne on the breeze.

Fargo breathed deeply of the dank forest scent and was at peace. He hiked another ten yards and unexpectedly emerged from the dense growth onto a clearly defined path that paralleled the road. Even more unexpected was the old woman walking down the path toward him. A faded homespun dress clung to her spindly frame, and she walked with the aid of a bent cane. She slowed in surprise, but only for a second.

"How do you do, young man? You startled me, coming out of nowhere like that."

Fargo smiled and said, "I'm not the Sangamon River Monster, if that's what you're thinking."

Her gray eyebrows puckered. "The what?"

"The Sangamon River Monster," Fargo said. "The man who has been killing people in these parts for the past ten years."

The old woman tilted her head and regarded him as if he might be addlepated. "Sonny, as the Lord is my witness, I never heard of the fella."

10

Arthur Draypool had an explanation. "I don't know who the old woman was, but the elderly tend to be feebleminded."

"Her mind was as sharp as yours or mine." Fargo had questioned the woman closely, and although she had lived in Illinois all her life, she could not recall so much as a single mention of the Sangamon River Monster.

"Maybe so," Draypool said. "But there's also the fact we're still well south of the Monster's usual haunts. Besides"—he paused and gestured at the thick greenery on both sides of the road—"it's not as if there are daily or weekly newspapers out here. Most news is spread by word of mouth." He paused again. "And didn't you say she lives all alone off in a cabin somewhere? If she doesn't have much contact with the outside world, how can you expect her to know about the Monster?"

Fargo supposed it was possible. The woman *had* told him she lived like a hermit, and liked it, because she had little hankering for human company.

"What exactly are you implying, anyhow?" Draypool demanded. "That there is no killer? That I went to considerable effort to find you, that I'm paying you a small fortune when you complete your task, as a lark?"

Fargo had to admit the notion was preposterous.

"Make no mistake," Draypool said earnestly. "I have never been more serious about anything in my life. I have pledged my heart, body, and soul to bringing the man we are after to bay. Whether you help us or not, I won't rest until I have accomplished what I have set out to do."

The rest of the afternoon was uneventful. They passed several cabins, and Fargo resisted an impulse to ask the occupants if they had ever heard of the killer. Draypool would not take it kindly.

Another night under the stars.

Fargo grew inwardly restive to find the Monster and get it over with. He reminded himself that for ten thousand dollars he could afford to be patient.

The next couple of days were spent wending to the northeast through a backwoodsman's paradise. A sign appeared, letting them know Springfield was ten miles ahead. Fargo was looking forward to a bath, a whiskey, and a woman, not necessarily in that order, and he was not happy when Arthur Draypool announced, "We will take the north fork when we come to it and go around Springfield, if you please, Mr. Zeck."

Fargo gigged the Ovaro up next to Draypool's animal. "Give me one good reason why we're not stopping."

"The fewer people who see us, the less likely that word will reach our quarry."

"No one knows who we are or what we are up to," Fargo said, more harshly than he intended. Being cautious was one thing. Draypool was taking it to an extreme.

"And I want to keep it that way. We are now in the heart of the killer's territory. We must not leave anything to chance."

Fargo had seen few men in buckskins since crossing into Illinois. His attire was bound to draw notice in Springfield, and while he did not see where it would do them any harm, he decided he would go along with what Draypool wanted.

This close to Springfield, homesteads were everywhere. Fargo lost count of the number of cabins and small houses they passed.

Then they topped a rise, and below stood a dwelling worthy of a king. Three stories high, it covered half an acre. The ground floor was composed of stone and mortar, the upper stories of hewn logs. A carriage shed and various other outbuildings were scattered about neatly maintained grounds, which were surrounded by a wrought-iron fence.

"Whoever lives there must have a lot of money," Fargo remarked.

"That he does." Arthur Draypool grinned. "Judge Oliver Harding is the gentleman's name, and he is doing us the singular honor of allowing us to stay at his home for the night."

"You don't say." Fargo wondered if Harding had a daughter. "He wouldn't happen to be another vigilante, would he?"

"Must you use that term? I find it most vulgar." Draypool sniffed. "But, yes, he is a member of our secret group. He also contributed a large amount to your fee."

"A judge who breaks the law when it suits him," Fargo commented. "What would folks say?"

Draypool frowned. "He does it for the common good, to save innocent lives."

"That's as good an excuse as any." Fargo was not sure why he was baiting Draypool. Maybe he was sick and tired of the whole secrecy business. Maybe it was resentment at how they were treating him. Or maybe it was both.

A wide gate barred entrance to the judge's estate. Stone columns supported the gate, and from behind the column on the left stepped a hawk-faced man holding a rifle. "That's far enough," he said. He was staring at Fargo, suspicion imprinted on his features. Then the guard noticed Draypool, and immediately his attitude changed. "Mr. Draypool! I didn't realize it was you, sir."

"A pleasure to see you again, Gerald."

Gerald gestured, and from behind the other stone column hastened another man to help him swing the heavy gate open.

Fargo let Draypool go ahead of him. Other guards were posted about the grounds, four that Fargo counted, with more probably out of sight. He wondered why the judge had a private little army.

Servants hurried out of the house to take the reins of their mounts and escort them indoors. All four wore brown uniforms with silver buttons. All four were black.

"And how are you, Akuda?" Draypool asked a fifth manservant, who waited by the front door.

"I am fine, sir. The judge has been expecting you, and your usual room is ready, as are rooms for these other gentlemen."

"You are an excellent butler, Akuda." Draypool smiled. "Someday I might take you away from Oliver."

"The judge would not permit that, sir. As he likes to say, we are his property now and forever."

Fargo had yet to meet Oliver Harding and already he did not think much of the man.

Draypool broke stride, and his face hardened in anger, but it was fleeting. He noticed Fargo watching him, and smiled at the butler. "Judge Harding has a marvelous sense of humor, does he not?"

"Certainly, sir," Akuda said politely.

The interior radiated wealth. The judge had a taste for luxury and bought only the best money could buy. Thick carpet cushioned Fargo's boots. He passed a marvelous painting of a waterfall and said, "Judges in Illinois must make more money than judges elsewhere."

Draypool did not take offense. "Oliver comes from a very old, very respected, and very rich family. I have known him for many years, and he is as fine a human being as you will ever meet."

Praise from a milksop, Fargo thought to himself, *is not much praise at all.* Aloud he said, "When do I get to meet him?"

"A good question," Draypool said. "What say you, Akuda?"

"The judge will be home by seven, sir," the butler answered. "Supper will be served promptly at seven thirty. If you require anything in the meantime, you have only to let me know."

They came to stairs and climbed. The banister was mahogany, the steps polished to a sheen.

Draypool was admitted to the first bedroom they came to. Avril and Zeck had to share the next. That left the bedroom at the end of the hall for Fargo. It was as comfortably furnished as the rest of the house. He dropped his saddlebags and the Henry onto the four-poster bed as Akuda went to the window and opened the curtains.

"If there is anything you need, sir, anything at all, I am at your service." He started for the doorway.

"I'd like to know a few things," Fargo said.

Akuda stopped. "What would they be, sir?"

"How long have you been a slave?"

The butler blinked. "All my life, sir, as was my father before me. Why do you ask?"

"The other servants—are they slaves as well?"

"Of course, sir," Akuda said in a tone that suggested it should be obvious. "The judge has many more at the family plantation in Alabama. He only moved here about five years ago."

"Do you know a man named Mayfair? Clyde Mayfair?"

"Yes, sir. He has stayed in this very house many times. He is a close friend of the judge's and Mr. Draypool's."

"The blacks who work in Mayfair's fields," Fargo said. "Are they slaves, too?"

"If you don't mind my saying so, sir, you ask strange questions," Akuda responded. "What else would they be? A lot of whites in Illinois own slaves, as do a lot of whites everywhere."

"Don't you want to be free?" Fargo asked. "To be your own man, and do as you please?"

Akuda let out a sigh. "Who would not? But I have learned not to yearn for that which we can never have. My dreams died when I was young."

"What can you tell me about the vigilantes?"

"The what, sir? I am not sure I understand."

"The group Draypool and the judge belong to," Fargo said. "The people who have hired me."

"The Secessionist League, sir? I know of no other group Judge Harding belongs to unless you count the club in Spring—". Akuda stopped. "Is something wrong, sir?"

The revelation had been like a slap to the face, causing Fargo to take an inadvertent step back. He remembered the so-called highwaymen, Frank Colter and Jim Sloane, and some of Sloane's last words: *But the government is on to you and the rest of the League. We won't let you light the fuse.*

"Sir?" Akuda said.

An awful feeling came over Fargo, a feeling that he had been played for a fool and had *been* one. "What can you tell me about the Sangamon River Monster?"

"The what, sir?"

"The killer who has been raiding homesteads for the past ten years. You must have heard of him."

"I'm sorry, sir. I know of no such person. Springfield is a peaceful place. There has not been a killing in years."

Fargo sat on the end of the bed and tucked his chin to his chest. He wished a tree were handy so he could beat his head against it.

"Is there anything else, sir?" Akuda inquired.

"No," Fargo said. "You've been a great help."

"I don't rightly see how," the butler said, and bowed as he backed out the door. He closed it after him.

Fargo's mind was in a whirl. He had heard of the Secessionist League but did not know a lot about it. Still, he could guess at its purpose. A lot of Southern states were unhappy with the federal government and there was talk on everyone's lips about the Southern states breaking away from the Union to form their own government. But what did the League want with him? Why had it gone to so much trouble to lure him to Illinois?

The longer Fargo pondered, the madder he became. He had been used, manipulated, led around like a bull with a ring in its nose. Fed lies and more lies. And all the while Arthur Draypool must have been chuckling as how easy he had been to dupe.

"The bastards," Fargo said aloud. He thought again of Colter and Sloane and came to the conclusion that they must have been government men assigned to keep an eye on the League. He hoped Colter had gotten away.

Fargo leaned back. A grim smile touched his lips. He would play along and see what happened. It was the only way to learn what the League was up to. Whatever it was, they would soon discover that baiting a wolf was dangerous.

A knock sounded. Standing, Fargo said gruffly, "Come in." He was expecting Draypool, but it was a petite young woman in a maid's outfit, a towel over her left arm.

"Sorry to disturb you, sir. Akuda says you need one of these." She moved toward a washbasin on a stand in the corner.

Fargo's interest perked. Her uniform hid a shapely body, evinced by the swell of her bosom and the sway of her hips. Her skin was a light coppery hue, her hair a velveteen black. Full lips in a perpetual pout complemented high cheekbones and alluring dark eyes. "Well, now," Fargo said. "Do you have a name or should I just call you Miss Beautiful?"

The maid grinned. "I am called Belda, sir. I will keep your room clean during your stay and make your bed in the morning." She placed the towel next to the basin and made to leave.

"I'll make my own," Fargo said, blocking her way. She stopped and looked up at him in frank appraisal.

"Is there something I can do for you, sir?"

"Stop calling me that," Fargo replied. "I'm not like the rest of the men here."

"If you say so, sir," Belda said. "Now, if you don't mind, I have other work to attend to." She moved to go around him.

"Wait," Fargo requested, taking hold of her arm. "I'd like to get together later, the two of us, somewhere private."

"I am not that kind of woman, sir," Belda said severely, prying his fingers off. "Please excuse me."

Fargo slid in front of her again. "It's not what you think. I need someone who can keep their ears open for me."

"I don't see what use I can be."

"Please," Fargo said, clasping her hand in appeal. "Where and when can I meet you?"

Half a minute went by. Then Belda said quietly, "They will punish me if I am caught, but I will meet you here at eleven tonight. Leave the door open slightly so I can slip inside."

"Thank you," Fargo said as she hustled to the hall. He smiled and walked to the washbasin. The Secessionist League had a lot to answer for and he was just the gent to see that it did.

11

The dining room was as luxurious as the rest of the house. A long table able to seat two dozen guests filled the center. Globe lamps at regular intervals provided brilliant illumination. The night was warm, and several windows were open to admit air.

The butler came for Fargo at seven fifteen. Fargo had availed himself of the washbasin, rummaged in his saddlebags for a clean bandanna, and wiped the dust from his boots. He wore his gun belt.

Akuda arched an eyebrow as Fargo stepped from the room, and said respectfully, "If you will forgive my presumption, sir, you will not require your firearm at the dinner table."

Fargo patted his holster. "I never go anywhere without it."

"The judge might take offense," Akuda said.

"You must have me confused with someone who gives a damn." Fargo smiled to lessen the sting.

"The judge likes to have his way," Akuda warned. "Trust me when I say he makes for a powerful enemy."

"I bet a lot of his enemies are against slavery." Fargo fished for information.

The butler broke stride, but only slightly. "The judge and his friends are very set in their beliefs."

"A Yankee hater, is he?"

Akuda glanced the length of the hall, then said

softly, "I should not discuss this with you, sir. The judge would be mad."

"What is the worst he can do to you?" Fargo asked half jokingly. He figured it would be a harsh lecture and extra work.

"He can have me whipped, sir," Akuda said, "and I would rather not go through that again, if you don't mind. I still have the scars from the other times."

Fargo envisioned the butler stripped to the waist, a whip biting into the flesh of his back. "Did the judge whip you himself?"

"Oh, no, sir, he would never sully his hands with someone else's blood. Mr. Garvey, the overseer from the judge's plantation, does the punishing." Akuda's frame seemed to tremble slightly. "You will meet him tonight."

"The overseer is here?"

"Yes, sir. Mr. Garvey comes up from Alabama every two or three months, sir, to consult with the judge. Sometimes he brings new staff for the house."

"New slaves, you mean," Fargo said.

Akuda nodded. "Or he takes those who have not been doing their jobs well enough to suit the judge back to Alabama to work in the fields."

"He's not the forgiving type, is he?"

Akuda uttered a laugh that was more like a bark. "Not at all, sir. The judge has a saying he is fond of." He paused. "Spare the rod, spoil the black."

Fargo tried to imagine what it must be like for the slaves, living in a constant state of fear, terrified to make a single mistake. "It's not right," he remarked, more to himself than the butler.

"There are a lot of things in this world that aren't right, sir," Akuda responded. "Things people shouldn't do to one another but do." They came to the stairs and he started down. "It makes me mad to this day that an accident of birth has made me what I am."

"That's natural."

Akuda went on talking without seeming to hear. "You have no idea what blacks have to put up with. Whites look down their noses at us because of the color of our skin. They treat us like we are not human, as if we are animals to be herded together and worked as they please."

"Not all whites think that way," Fargo said.

"Enough do," Akuda said. "Enough to make our lives miserable. Enough that many of my kind would rather they had never been born." They were almost to the bottom, and he leaned toward Fargo and pleaded, "Please, sir, not a word about our talk to anyone."

"Don't worry." Fargo clapped him on the back. "They couldn't pry it out of me with burning coals."

Arthur Draypool was already at the table. So were three others. One was a human mountain dressed in an ill-fitting suit. Close to seven feet tall, he had short blond hair, a clipped yellow beard, and obsidian eyes that fixed on Fargo with baleful intensity. That would be Garvey, Fargo guessed.

Across from the overseer sat a plump woman in her middle years, her dress much too tight for her bulk, her bosom threatening to burst the fabric if she exhaled too strongly. She had a pumpkin head and tiny seed eyes. "Mr. Fargo," she said, offering her pudgy hand. "I am Winifred Harding, the judge's wife. I am sorry I was not here to greet you when you arrived, but I was in Springfield most of the day."

Her skin was dry and smelled of powder. Fargo stepped past her to an empty chair. Across from him was the other new face, a woman only half as old as Winifred and not half as heavy, but otherwise the family resemblance was plain. "You must be the judge's daughter."

"Not quite. I am his niece," she said in a sultry tone. "Darby Harding," she introduced herself. "My father is the judge's younger brother. I came up from the South with Mr. Garvey to pay my uncle a visit."

Garvey grunted. "Heard a lot about you, mister." He held out a hand the size of a bear paw. "Hope you turn out to be everything the judge and his friends expect."

"The Sangamon River Monster is as good as caught," Fargo said to gauge how they reacted. He received smiles and the sort of expressions professional gamblers wore when they were fleecing the gullible.

"I love a man with confidence," Winifred Harding declared in a much friendlier tone than was warranted.

Fargo was more interested in the niece, who met his frank stare with one of her own. "How long are you staying?"

"For as long as my uncle needs me," Darby said. "Uncle Oliver and I have always been close. I would do anything for him."

At that juncture, into the dining room marched their host. Harding was as plump as his wife except for his face, which had the hard, angular lines of a black-smith's anvil. He came around the table without so much as a nod of acknowledgment to anyone, including his wife. Akuda held out a chair for him and he sat in it as if sitting on a throne. "I trust I haven't kept all of you waiting too long."

"Not at all, Uncle," Darby said.

"You are punctual, as always," Winifred chorused. "And even if you were not, we would gladly wait."

Fargo sensed a strange sort of competition between them. He focused on the judge, absorbing details: piercing brown eyes, black hair going to gray, an aura of authority that Fargo normally saw in military officers.

"Nonsense, my dear," Oliver Harding declared. "It would be a poor host indeed who kept his guests wait-ing." He was looking at his niece as he spoke. "My dearest Darby. How wonderfully you grace our table. It is a shame you don't visit us more often."

Winifred Harding squirmed in her chair like a worm squirming on a hook. "Yes, we always look forward to having you, my dear."

The judge swiveled. "Arthur! I trust there were no difficulties on your trip. You must tell me everything over brandies later."

Fargo could not resist. "We ran into a pair of outlaws on our way here. Or highwaymen, as you would call them."

Oliver Harding became a stone statue. Then he said, with no trace of emotion whatsoever, "On behalf of the state of Illinois, I apologize. We are not yet as civilized as our brethren to the east. We have not yet tamed the wilder element among us." He smiled without warmth. "And you, I take it, are the famous Trailsman. It is an honor to make your acquaintance."

"Yes, it is, isn't it?" Winifred Harding said.

The judge clapped his hands, and at the signal, servants began filing in bearing food. Fargo filled his plate with venison, potatoes, green beans, and a thick slice of bread layered with butter. He did not have much of an appetite, but on the frontier he had learned to eat when he could because he never knew how long it would be between meals. Especially lavish meals like this one.

Judge Harding and Arthur Draypool did most of the talking, with the judge's wife making occasional comments. Most of it was of no interest, having to do with recent cases the judge had presided over, their mutual friend Clyde Mayfair, and the general lawlessness.

Fargo suspected that last was for his benefit. He had seen no evidence of it on the way there. Everyone they met had been friendly and seemed law-abiding. But he kept his suspicions private. He would let them go on thinking they had pulled the wool over his eyes.

Midway through the meal a commotion arose in the hall, and presently Akuda ushered in a man who had the dust of many miles on his clothes and a quirt in his hand. The new arrival whispered in Judge Harding's ear, and the judge excused himself, saying he must attend to personal business.

Fargo pretended not to notice the pointed glances Draypool and Garvey cast his way. He began to wash down his supper with a cup of piping-hot coffee, flavored with a pinch of sugar.

In due course the judge returned. His mood had completely changed. Where before he was reserved and cold, he came back in whistling merrily, a new spring in his step.

"Good news?" Fargo asked between sips.

"Yes, indeed," Judge Harding replied. "A critical business arrangement has turned out better than we dared hope." When he said "we," he glanced out of the corner of an eye at Arthur Draypool. He did it so quickly, and so cleverly, that only someone whose vision had been honed to the razor sharpness of a hawk's in order to survive in the peril-filled fastness of the mountains and the vast plains would catch it.

Darby was toying with her green beans. "So tell me, Mr. Fargo," she ventured, "how do you rate your prospects of catching the killer?"

"I can track anything that lives," Fargo said matter-of-factly.

"Then that terrible man is as good as caught!" Winifred Harding declared. "You will be doing the whole world a service by helping to eliminate him."

"The whole world?" Fargo repeated.

Judge Harding waved a hand in his Winifred's direction but did not look at her. "Forgive her. My wife has a flair for the dramatic. By the whole world she means Illinois, which is her whole world, in a sense."

Fargo reminded himself that most judges were lawyers, and lawyers were masters of twisting phrases to suit them.

"Yes, that's what I meant," Winifred said, bobbing her double chins. "Please don't read more into what I say than there is."

Judge Harding made a tepee of his fingers. "I suggest it is time for the ladies to retire to the drawing room so the men can smoke their cigars."

Winifred came out of her chair as if someone had poked her bottom with a pin. "Oh. Certainly. Whatever you want, dearest. Belda will bring us our desserts."

The judge and Draypool slid cigars from inner pockets and proceeded to clip the ends and light them, an elaborate ritual that ended with both of them leaning back, blowing smoke toward the ceiling, and sighing contentedly.

"There is nothing quite like a good cigar after a hard day's work," Judge Harding observed. He offered one to Fargo, but Fargo declined. "You don't smoke? Pity. You're depriving yourself of one of life's too few joys."

"I don't smoke, either," Garvey said. The overseer had voiced only a few comments all evening.

"You should," Arthur Draypool said. "Tobacco is God's gift to humankind. Unlike alcohol, it doesn't have any bad effects."

"Unless you count accidentally setting your clothes on fire when you light up," Judge Harding joked.

Fargo did not share in their chuckles. "Tell me more about the Monster," he urged Harding. "Has anyone ever made a list of the names of all those he's butchered?"

"I have the information right here." Judge Harding tapped his temple. "His first victims were the Myrtle family, ten years ago next month. They were from Rhode Island. They came here to farm and were buried on their plot."

"I remember them," Arthur Draypool said. "In addition to the parents, there were two small girls and a small boy, correct?"

"That was the family, yes," the judge said. "I presided at the burials. Little did we realize more atrocities would follow."

Fargo had to hand it to them. They lied as slickly as patent medicine salesmen. "Who were some of the others?"

Judge Harding related the deaths of victim after victim, adding little touches about their appearance and what they supposedly did for a living to make it more believable. "As you can see," he said, summing things up, "my wife was not all that remiss about how badly we need your help."

It was well past nine when Harding and Draypool excused themselves and headed upstairs, the judge commenting, "It would be wise if you gentlemen did the same. Tomorrow may well be the day we receive news of the Monster's whereabouts."

Fargo left the dining room. The shadow that fell across him as he came to the upstairs landing was as big as the shadow of a redwood.

"I look forward to working with you," Garvey said.

"I work alone."

"Not against the Monster you don't," Garvey responded. "Mr. Harding and Mr. Draypool told me we are sticking with you." He stopped at a room. "This is mine. See you in the morning."

Fargo shook off a feeling of a net closing around him. His uneasiness resurfaced, and he latched his bedroom door. Sprawling out on his back, he was on the verge of dozing off when a light knock sounded. The clock on the wall said it was five minutes to eleven. Belda was early. He threw the latch and pulled the door wide, and could not hide his surprise.

"I thought you might like some company," Darby Harding said.

12

A wariness came over Fargo. He was unsure why. Darby was not armed and posed no threat. Quite the opposite. She was dressed for bed, in a gown that clung to her as if it had been painted on, accenting her enticing charms.

Fargo remembered how eagerly Priscilla Mayfair had thrown herself into his arms at the Mayfair farm, and the feeling came over him that this was the exact same situation. Which suggested there was more here than met his eye. He had a sudden conviction that the two women did not necessarily cozy up to him by choice, which meant someone had put Priscilla and now Darby up to it.

"Are you going to let me in or must I stand out here making a horse's ass of myself?"

Fargo glanced down the hall. He saw no one, but his instincts told him they were being watched and his instincts were seldom wrong. "It's late and I'm tired."

Darby's features rippled in astonishment. "You would rather go to bed alone? Are you the real Skye Fargo or an impostor? The real Fargo, I've heard, has slept with more women than the entire Fifth Cavalry." She laughed lightly and splayed fragrant fingers on his chest. "You're not serious, are you?"

The cleavage she displayed would have weakened a monk's resolve, and Fargo was no monk. "Afraid so," he said, and started to close the door.

"No, you don't." Darby barged past him, her eyes flashing with anger. "I won't have it thrown in my face."

Fargo nearly grabbed her by the arm and shoved her back out. He did not like being used. He never had. "What?" he asked.

"The gift I'm offering you," Darby said, and gestured at her soft, sinewy body with all its glorious attributes. "If you make me leave it will be an insult."

"I'm not in the mood," Fargo said, and smirked at the thought that he had never in his life said that to a woman before.

Darby stepped to the bed and turned, one leg visible in the folds of her robe, revealing velvet skin from her toes to her thigh. "Don't give me that. Men are always in the mood. They are born randy and get worse as they get older."

"Not all men," Fargo quibbled. He left the door open and leaned against the jamb. "Besides, women like it just as much as men. They like to put on airs and pretend they don't, but they do."

"Is that so?" Darby slid more of her leg out of the robe. She waited, and when he did not say or do anything, she gestured again, angrily. "If you know so much about women, you should know that we don't like having our airs, or our needs, treated with contempt."

Fargo wondered how far she would push. And was it her uncle, or Draypool, who was behind the charade?

Darby softened and forced a thin smile. "Let's start over, shall we? I don't suppose you have something to drink? I sure could use a brandy right about now."

Fargo stretched, and yawned.

"Damn you. You're making me mad." Darby tapped her foot with impatience. "This isn't what I expected."

"Next time don't take things for granted," Fargo said.

"There won't be a next time, mister," Darby snapped. "I don't care what they—" She caught herself, and stopped.

Fargo folded his arms across his chest. She had said "they." He wanted to ask who "they" were, but he must not act too suspicious or they would guess that he knew they were up to something. He must continue to act the fool. "Look. It's been a long day. I'm tired. I would like to catch some sleep."

"What's one more hour or so?" Darby asked suggestively. Her breasts jiggling like ripe fruit on a tree limb, she sashayed toward him. "I'll make it worth your while. I promise."

Her anger had faded, but now Fargo's flared. He was sick and tired of being manipulated like a puppet on a string. The Secessionist League had a reckoning coming. But he could not make his move until they made theirs.

"Well, big man?" Darby stopped and taunted him with her gaze and her posture. She was a gumdrop and he was a kid staring into the jar in the general store. "See something you like?"

"These," Fargo said, and reaching out with both hands, he covered her mounds and squeezed, hard. Really hard.

Darby stiffened and arched her back. She bit her lower lip to stifle an outcry, then covered his hands with hers and said throatily, "Not so rough, if you please. That hurts."

"Does it?" Fargo pinched her nipples, none too gently.

"Ah!" Darby threw her head back and took half a step backward, but she could not escape his grasp. Her entire face reddened and she gasped, "Shut the door! We don't want anyone to see us."

"You shut it if you want," Fargo said, but as she started to step past him he flicked a hand between her legs and up under her robe.

"What are you—?" Darby blurted. "Oh!" She tried to pull back, but his fingers were where he wanted them. "The bed, damn you. Carry me to the bed."

"Why bother?" Fargo slowly lowered his mouth to her neck and bit her. As his teeth sank in, he thrust upward with his middle finger.

"Ah! Dear God!" Darby placed her hands on his shoulders and feebly attempted to push him away, but another thrust buckled her knees and she sagged against him, groaning deep in her throat. "Not like this," she whispered.

"Why not?" Fargo lowered her left hand to his pants.

"Ohhhhh." Trembling, Darby closed her eyes. Her forehead dipped to his chest and she panted uncontrollably, caught in the throes of lust. "This isn't how I wanted it to be."

"Didn't you?" Fargo wrapped his free arm around her waist and lifted. She did not weigh much, no more than a hundred and ten or so, and he easily raised her high enough. She looked at him quizzically, not divining his intent until she felt movement below their waists.

"What are you doing?" Darby jerked at the contact. "Not like this! Not standing up when there is a bed right there!"

"I like to stand," Fargo teased, and did with his hips as he had been doing with his fingers.

"No! No! No!" Darby protested huskily, but her body was saying *yes, yes, yes*! She enfolded him like a sheath and held herself still, scarcely breathing. "I don't think I like you very much," she said in a tiny voice.

"I don't like you much either," Fargo responded, and rose up onto the tips of his toes.

A whine issued from Darby's full lips, a whine of

commingled need and frustration. She thrashed from side to side as if she were in pain, but her expression betrayed the carnal truth.

Suddenly turning, Fargo pressed her against the wall. They were inches from the open door, and the hallway. Anyone coming down it could not fail to notice them. "Maybe we'll have an audience," he said.

"You are the worst bastard I have ever met," Darby growled. "I should claw your eyes out."

"You're welcome to try." Fargo rammed up into her with all his might. She choked off a shriek as her body went into a paroxysm of rapture. Her legs hiked upward and wrapped tight around him.

"I will hate you for this."

"I'll try not to lose sleep over it," was Fargo's retort. He cupped her breasts and kneaded them like clay he was trying to rip apart.

"That hurts!" Darby mewed, her eyelids hooded, her chest heaving.

"Do you want me to stop?"

"Yes! No! I mean—" Darby gasped. "I didn't figure on this! I like tenderness. I like— Oh!" She shuddered, and at his next thrust, flung her arms around him and clung desperately to his shoulder. "No! Don't stop! I want it! God help me, I want it, I want it, I want it."

"Then you can have it." Fargo unleashed the full power of his need, slamming repeatedly into her. His manhood and her womanhood were a fluid meld—his hard to her soft, his sword to her scabbard, his ram to her ewe. She no longer cared that the door was open, no longer cared that someone was secretly spying on them or that someone else might happen by. She was lost in the moment. He lost himself in it, too, giving himself entirely to his craving.

Fargo heard her whimper. Later she might harbor regrets, but he felt no prick of conscience. She had brought it on herself. He drove into her yet again and she sucked in a breath that seemed to have no end while quaking in the throes of raw abandon.

"I'm almost there!"

So was Fargo. His throat was constricted and his skin tingled. A tight sensation in his groin heralded his impending eruption, but he gritted his teeth and held off, thinking of the wall, the ceiling, the house, anything and everything except his body, and the throbbing.

"Ahhhhhhh!" Darby was at the pinnacle. Her eyes grew wide. She dug her nails in, and crested. Up and down, up and down, her body a lever, his the fulcrum. She gushed and gushed, and he did the same.

After a while Darby slowly disentangled herself and wearily stepped back. Her robe and undergarments were in disarray, her hair a mess. "I would like to put a bullet in your brain."

Fargo adjusted his pants and his belt, and stepped aside. "Stop by anytime," he said, and motioned at the doorway. Her hand was a blur, but he caught her wrist and held fast. "I don't deserve that. You got what you came for."

Tugging futilely to be free, Darby hissed, "I hate you! You're a crude lout! A buffoon in buckskins!"

"Yet you made love to me."

Darby's features twisted into rage. She started to swing her other hand but thought better of it and with a visible effort of will, slowly relaxed, her venom subsiding but still there, just under the surface. "Let go of me, please. I would like to go to my room."

Fargo did as she requested, but she stood there rubbing her wrist. "Do you want me to carry you?"

A sly smile came over her. "If you only knew what is in store, you would appreciate my gift."

"I'm grateful for what you've done," Fargo said, but he was referring to the slip of her tongue that confirmed his hunch about Priscilla and her.

Darby sidled past. She traced a finger across his jaw,

saying, "When you are out there in the deep woods, think of me." She paused to smooth her robe and fuss with her hair. "I will say one thing in your favor. If you track like you make love, then the man you are after is as good as snared." She blew him a kiss and walked off.

Fargo watched her until she came to another door. It was open a crack. As she reached out, the door opened, and there was shadowy movement. She smiled at whoever was inside, said something, and went in.

Fargo shut his own door and plopped onto his back on the bed. The long day in the saddle, the meal, the interlude with Darby, all conspired to fill him with lassitude. He succumbed, drifting into a deep sleep.

He was unsure of exactly how much time had passed when he suddenly found himself awake, his eyes wide open. Something had snapped him out of dreamland. He probed with his senses, trying to identify the cause, and heard sounds from the front of the house.

Rising, he padded to the hall. Other doors were opening. From one stepped Arthur Draypool in an ankle-length nightshirt. From another came Garvey, wearing pants and nothing else. Darby emerged next, stifling a yawn and blinking in the glow of the hall lamp.

"What's all the ruckus?" Garvey asked. "It's four o'clock in the morning."

"I was having the most marvelous dream," Draypool said. "I was back in South Carolina, revisiting the haunts of my youth."

A loud, gruff voice rose to the rafters from downstairs. "Bring him in!" Judge Harding bawled. "I will speak with him immediately."

Fargo followed the rest to the landing. At the foot of the stairs stood the judge in a bulky robe, Winifred at his side. The butler, Akuda, was hurrying down the entryway to the front door. There was a subdued exchange, and Akuda reappeared, leading a tall man in garb that marked him as a backwoodsman: a hat made from a raccoon pelt, including the tail, a buckskin shirt, and jeans. He removed his hat out of deference to Winifred.

"Bill Layton?" Judge Harding said. "What is the meaning of this outrageous disturbance at such an ungodly hour?"

Layton wrung his hat. "My apologies, Your Honor. Word is that you wanted to be informed right away if the Sangamon River Monster struck again. Any time of the day or night." The man talked strangely, in a stilted cadence that suggested he was speaking by rote.

Fargo was puzzled, until it occurred to him that the whole incident had been concocted for his benefit.

Judge Harding was playing his part. "There has been an attack?" he asked, much more loudly than was warranted.

"Yes, sir. Early this evening a family of four was butchered on a farm ten miles north of Springfield. It's terrible. Just terrible. Like all the rest of the Sangamon River Monster's handiwork."

"I'm sorry for the family, but the timing could not be more perfect," Judge Harding said. "At last that madman has made a mistake we can capitalize on."

Winifred had a plump hand to her throat, holding her nightgown close. "You're going after him, I take it, dearest?"

"I must," Judge Harding declared, "but I'm not going alone, so set your mind at rest." He stabbed a finger at the butler. "Akuda, go wake Arthur and Fargo. Garvey, too, while you are at it."

Draypool leaned over the banister to holler, "We are already up, Oliver! Give us ten minutes and we will be ready to depart." He beamed at Fargo. "Can you believe our luck? Your first night here and you will have a crack at the Monster."

"It's too good to be true," Fargo said.

13

It was called Old Woman Creek. A tributary of the Sangamon River, it was so far into the forest that few whites had ever set eyes on it. In recent months, though, a handful of hardy settlers had established homesteads on its grassy banks and were struggling to eke out an existence.

The Sweeney family had been one of them. A burly father with features as rugged as the land he cleared, a mother stout of body and given to hanging crosses on every wall, a boy of fifteen, on the verge of manhood, and a girl of twelve, sweet and innocent and dressed in white.

Their bodies had been left where they fell. As near as Fargo could reconstruct the sequence of events, the father had been chopping wood with his back to the forest and someone had slunk up behind him and caved in his skull. In falling, the man had reached for a rifle he had leaned against the woodpile, the instinctive, last act of a father wanting to protect his loved ones.

The mother must have been watching out a window and seen her husband die. Her body lay a few yards outside the cabin, a pistol only inches from her right hand. She had been shot in the chest. Fargo picked up the pistol and examined it. None of the cartridges in the cylinder had been fired.

The boy had rushed out to help them and been

killed in the doorway, the top of his head blown off. Fargo had to step over the body to go inside.

In a corner near the fireplace lay the girl. She had been stabbed, not shot. Stabbed repeatedly. Scarlet stains marked her white dress in front and in back, indicating the killer had continued to stab her after she fell. From the blood on her fingers and her torn fingernails, Fargo could determine that she had fought fiercely for her life.

All the bodies had been mutilated. Their ears had been sliced off, and were missing. Trophies, apparently, as were random missing fingers and thumbs, and in the case of the mother, her nose. The father's face had been kicked in. The son's genitals were gone. Fargo had to turn away from the things done to the girl. Hideous things inflicted by a hideous mind.

"What did I tell you?" Arthur Draypool said as Fargo walked toward the door. "The murderer is as vile a human being as ever existed."

Judge Harding nudged the boy's body with his polished boot. "How can you call someone who could do this human? He's a monster, and aptly named."

Fargo breathed deep of the humid air. It had taken them half a day to get there; the judge, Arthur Draypool, Avril and Zeck, the overseer, Garvey, the man called Layton who had brought word of the slaughter, and four others who had not said a single word the entire ride. Fargo had ridden near the front of the group, with Draypool and Harding, and had not had much of a chance to study the four who had been at the rear. He studied them now.

They were cut from the same coarse cloth. Backwoodsmen, homespun and buckskins their attire. All but one wore badly scuffed boots or shoes. The last wore knee-high moccasins and was further different from the others in that he was completely clad in buckskins and wore a beaded buckskin bag slanted across his chest. The man had lived with Indians at one time, Fargo guessed, and had taken up some Indian ways.

They bristled with weapons: rifles, pistols, knives, tomahawks. Haughty in manner, they met his scrutiny with arrogant stares. Hard men who had lived hard lives and bowed to no one. That they had been waiting outside the judge's house with Layton hinted to Fargo that they had arrived with him. He had assumed they were acquaintances of the slain family, but now he suspected otherwise. Backwoodsmen were a tough breed, but they were generally friendly. There was nothing friendly about these four.

"Whenever you are ready to begin tracking," Judge Harding urged, "by all means, get to it."

The clearing had been trampled. Someone—a lot of someones—had left a jumble of footprints, making it impossible to distinguish those of the Sangamon River Monster from the rest. Fargo mentioned as much to the judge and Draypool.

"Blame neighbors and friends and the curious from the hamlet of Carne, about four miles east of here," Harding said. "They were unaware I wanted the scene preserved. But don't despair. Layton tells me he has found the Monster's trail." The judge crooked a finger and Layton came at a run. "Show him," Harding commanded.

The killer had headed northeast through the forest. His tracks were as plain as tracks could be, especially since he had made no effort to conceal them. That struck Fargo as peculiar. He knelt to examine a set in a patch of bare earth, reading them as other people read the print in books.

The killer had big feet. He wore shoes, not boots or moccasins, which Fargo also found peculiar. According to Draypool and Harding, the Monster lived off in the deep woods somewhere, and men who did that invariably chose moccasins or boots over common shoes. The edges of the heels and sole were clearly defined, another peculiarity. It meant the shoes were fairly new, for the heels and soles had not worn down from prolonged use.

Going by the depth of the prints, Fargo figured the killer weighed about the same as he did. The length of the killer's stride was longer, though, which told Fargo the man had longer legs, which suggested the killer was taller than Fargo, and consequently slighter of build. Lean and lanky was how Fargo would describe him.

"Well?" Arthur prompted.

Fargo rose. Draypool and the judge and the others had come over and were waiting expectantly. "Well, what?"

"Why are you dawdling? We hired you to track him, remember? Be on your way. Precious daylight is being squandered."

Turning toward the Ovaro, Fargo said, "When I find him I'll take him alive. What you do after that is up to you."

"Hold on," the judge said. "We want someone to go with you."

"No," Fargo said.

"Be reasonable." From Draypool.

"I work alone. I told you that." Fargo rarely made exceptions. He took a step, but Arthur snagged his arm.

"Hear us out. Is that too much to ask for ten thousand dollars?"

"You're squandering precious daylight," Fargo reminded him.

Judge Harding clenched his fists. "Be that as it may, as your employers we have a stake in the outcome, and the right to speak our minds." He waved a fist in the direction of the log cabin. "As God is my witness, those will be the Monster's last victims."

"We can't leave anything to chance," Draypool said. "What if something were to happen to you?"

Fargo went to respond, and Draypool held up a hand. "I know, I know. You can take care of yourself. No one questions your ability. But accidents occur. Things don't always go as we want them to go. If anything happened to you, how would we know? You might track the Monster to his lair and be unable to get word to us. Then all this will have been for naught."

Reluctantly, Fargo had to admit he had a point.

"What we propose is this: Take one man with you. Just one." Draypool pointed at Bill Layton. "He is to do whatever you ask of him at all times. When you find where the killer is holed up, Layton will keep watch while you hurry and fetch us." He smiled hopefully. "Isn't that reasonable?"

"I suppose," Fargo said.

That was when the man wearing the knee-high moccasins declared in a distinct Southern drawl, "It shouldn't be Layton. It should be me."

"We want Layton," Draypool said.

"I'm better," the man said. "Faster, stronger, the best damn shot you have. It's a mistake to use him."

"We have been all through this," Judge Harding interjected. "We need you with us. Bill is perfectly capable of doing what we require. He knows our wishes."

Layton nodded.

"Suit yourselves," the man in the knee-high moccasins said. "But don't blame me if it doesn't go as you hope."

Fargo noticed that Draypool was intimidated by the man, perhaps even a little afraid, and that Judge Harding, who kowtowed to no one, treated him with a degree of deference. There was more to this one than was apparent.

"Layton it is, then," Draypool said. Then, to Fargo, "Is there anything you require before you head out? Food? Ammo? Anything at all?"

"I'm all set." Fargo always lived off the land when he was on the go. His needs were few.

"And you?" Draypool said to Layton.

"I bought supplies just last week. I'm as ready as I'll ever be."

"Excellent. Then off the two of you go. Remember, we want to catch the Monster before he strikes again. But you must not be so hasty that you lose him. There might not be another opportunity like this for many months."

"I won't lose him," Fargo vowed. Once he was on a manhunt, he never let up. The only time two-legged quarry had ever eluded him had been in New Mexico, and the quarry had been a Mimbres Apache. In Fargo's opinion, Apaches were the best trackers anywhere, and were equally adept at shaking whoever attempted to track them.

"We are counting on you," Judge Harding said. "More than you can ever know." In a rare display of emotion, he put a hand on Fargo's shoulder. "A lot is riding on you, but I am confident you won't disappoint us."

Fargo was glad to get out of there. He held the Ovaro to a walk in order to read the sign. He assumed the killer had a mount hidden in the woods, but after half a mile he came to the conclusion the man had been afoot. Exactly what Arthur Draypool had said the Monster would do.

Except for slight deviations to avoid obstacles like logs and boulders, the killer's course was a beeline toward some unknown destination. And from his stride, the Monster was in a hurry to get there, moving at a steady, tireless jog.

Layton hung back, presumably in the belief that Fargo wanted nothing to do with him. But Fargo could talk and track at the same time, and there were questions that begged answers. "How long have you worked for Harding?" he asked over his shoulder.

"Seven years this—"

Layton stopped, and Fargo could guess why. They

wanted him to think Layton had just happened upon the massacre and rushed to inform the judge.

"Did you ask how long have I known him?"

"Worked for," Fargo said.

"Oh. I didn't quite hear you. I'm not in the judge's employ. I have a homestead near Carne, with a wife and five kids."

If Layton was married, Fargo was the queen of England. "Doesn't it worry you, them alone with the killer on the loose?"

"My wife has a good head on her shoulders, and can shoot the bull's-eye out of a target at a hundred paces."

"You must want the killer caught as much as the judge and the rest of his vigilantes do," Fargo remarked.

"Don't call them that. They are patriots. They do what is best for the common good with no thought of reward for themselves."

Once again, Fargo had the feeling Layton was repeating someone else's comments. "You think highly of them."

"I think highly of the cause. I was born in these parts, but that doesn't mean I can't share their beliefs."

The undergrowth grew thicker. Fargo had to thread the Ovaro through it like a giant black-and-white needle through a green tapestry. Locusts droned in the trees. A pair of young squirrels scampered about in the leafy boughs. A blue jay shrieked and took swift wing.

To Fargo, the sights and sounds of the wild were always a tonic. They filled him to overflowing with a sense of being alive. Some men were so soured on life they could not get the acid out of their system, but not Fargo. To him each day was a feast of new experiences waiting over the next horizon.

"Mind if I ask you a question?" Layton broke a long silence.

"Depends on what it is," Fargo said, suddenly wary. He must not do or say anything that would give away the fact that he suspected he was being used as a tool by the Secessionist League.

"Folks say you have killed more men than Samson. Is that true?"

"You shouldn't believe everything you hear." Fargo reined to the left to go around blackberry bushes, with their sharp thorns.

"I don't mind that you're a killer," Layton said. "Hell, a lot of people have blood on their hands but keep it secret. I've killed once or twice myself."

"And here we are, tracking another killer," Fargo said.

"You can't hardly compare him to us. He's a butcher. He murders people for the fun of it. You and me, we only kill when we have to."

For Fargo that was true. He was not so sure about Layton. "Killing is killing, some would say, and accuse us of being no better than the Monster."

"Nonsense!" Layton spat. "Anyone too stupid to see the difference deserves to have their throat slit."

Fargo could not help but grin.

"It depends on why people kill," Layton went on. "Their motive, as the judge calls it. He says that some motives are higher than others, and the highest of all is to kill for an honorable cause."

"Interesting notion," Fargo said.

"The judge is a great man. He has a vision for the future. One day soon that vision will come true and this country will be a better place."

"What kind of vision?"

Perhaps aware he had said too much, Layton hesitated, then answered, "You should ask him. He's a better talker than me."

"You admire him a lot, I gather?" Fargo trolled for information.

"I admire the cause," Layton said, and quickly

amended, "That is, I believe in bringing murderers to justice."

Fargo thought of the Sweeney family, and the young girl crumpled in a corner of their cabin, her white dress stained scarlet from multiple stab wounds. "That makes two of us."

14

The killer's endurance was worthy of an Apache's. Mile after mile through some of the heaviest vegetation Fargo had ever encountered, the man held to a remarkable pace. Many times Fargo had to dismount and lead the Ovaro by the reins. The press of growth demanded it.

Layton did not say much. He always hung back and let Fargo lead, which was to be expected. But Fargo did not like having the man behind him. Now and again the skin on his back itched, and he would tell himself that he was being silly. Layton wouldn't shoot him or do whatever the judge and Draypool had ordered him to do until they caught up to the Sangamon River Monster.

Night found them no closer to their quarry. Fargo made camp in a small clearing. He kindled a fire and put coffee on to brew. Their meal consisted of pemmican on his part and jerky on Layton's.

They were sipping their first steaming cup when Layton cleared his throat and asked, "What's it like out there?"

Fargo knew what he meant but asked, "Out where?"

"Out west. We hear so many stories. Are the Indians as fierce and bloodthirsty as everyone says?"

"Some Indians," Fargo said, "but no more so than some whites."

"They say you've lived with Indians."

"Who does?"

Layton shrugged. "Oh, people I've talked to in taverns and the like."

"People talk too damn much." Fargo was in an irritable mood. It rankled him, being used.

"Do they ever. But don't get me wrong. I wouldn't hold it against you. I know another man who has lived with Indians. Some tribe down in Florida. He dresses like an Indian and acts half Indian all the time."

"This man have a name?" Fargo asked without really caring.

"Hiram Trask. I doubt you have ever heard of him. He's not anywhere near as famous as you are."

Fargo's gut tightened. *Could it be?* he asked himself. "I have heard of him. He's supposed to be a damn good tracker."

"One of the best," Layton said. "Folks say he can track an ant across solid rock, but folks exaggerate."

"That they do," Fargo agreed amiably. Then, as casually as possible, he blew on the coffee and said, "I've heard Trask is partial to knee-high moccasins."

Layton chuckled and said, "He wears the silly things all the time. Once in Georgia we went into a fancy restaurant with him wearing them and everyone stared—" Layton froze, his cup halfway to his mouth.

"So that was Hiram Trask," Fargo said. "Strange he didn't introduce himself. Or that Draypool or Harding didn't mention him."

"Hiram's not much of a talker." Layton tried to undo the damage. "And Mr. Draypool and the judge probably figured you wouldn't understand."

"Understand what?" Fargo shammed. "That two trackers working together are better than one? Trask should be with us."

Beads of sweat had broken out on Layton's brow. "Maybe the judge wants Hiram handy in case something happens to you."

"That could be." Fargo enjoyed making him squirm.

"Or it could be Trask is part of the League, like you and Draypool and the judge."

Layton paled and nearly dropped his tin cup. "The what?"

"The Secessionist League. Why you went to all the trouble to hire me when you have Trask puzzles me."

"I don't know what you're talking about."

"Sure you don't," Fargo said. "Just like you don't know that there is no Sangamon River Monster and never has been. Just like you don't know that it was you and your friends who murdered the Sweeney family."

Layton sat stock-still. "You're ranting nonsense."

"And you're a terrible liar." Fargo made a mental stab in the dark. "When are you supposed to kill me? Or is Draypool leaving that up to Hiram Trask?"

"You must be drunk."

"Have you seen me take a drink all day?" Fargo countered, watching the backwoodsman's hands.

"What in God's name makes you think there's no Sangamon River Monster?"

"I've talked to people who have never heard of him."

"What's so peculiar about that?" Layton asked.

"Draypool claimed the killings have been going on for ten years," Fargo said. "Everyone in Illinois would know about them by now."

"Not necessarily." Layton pushed his raccoon hat back on his head. He seemed to be thinking furiously. His face lit, as if at inspiration, and he asked, "If the Sangamon River Monster doesn't exist, then whose tracks are we following?"

"I was hoping you would tell me," Fargo said. "Then you can go back and tell your bosses that whatever they are up to didn't work."

"I can't do that."

"Tell them, too, that I'll be coming for them. They must pay for the Sweeneys. Why that family, anyway?

Did Draypool and the judge pick them out of thin air? Or were they Northern sympathizers?"

Layton's eyes darted right and left, like those of an animal caught in a cage. "Sheer nonsense, I tell you."

"Keep it to yourself, then," Fargo said. "But now that things are out in the open, I'd like for you to hand me your revolver."

"What?"

"I don't keep rattlesnakes in my pocket, and I don't let men out to kill me keep the guns to do it with."

"Crazy as a loon," Layton declared.

Fargo extended his left hand, palm up. "Your revolver."

"Like hell! You have no right!" Layton started to stand but sat back down again. He was a study in nervousness. His jaw muscles twitched. He shifted his legs one way and then another.

"We don't have all night," Fargo said.

Like a punctured bladder deflating, Layton's body sagged and he said resignedly, "I'll give it to you. But once you realize the mistake you've made, I want it back. Understood?"

"You're stalling."

"All right, all right. Hold your horses." Layton set down his cup and lowered his right arm toward his Remington.

Fargo's gaze was glued to the other arm, to the hand that brushed Layton's hip. Cold steel flashed and lanced at his throat. With a deft twist of his wrist he threw his coffee into Layton's face even as he skipped to one side to evade the blade. He thought it would buy him the split second he needed to draw, but Layton was on him before his fingers could close on the Colt's grip. Again the knife speared at his jugular. He had to throw himself backward to save himself, and in doing so he tripped over his saddle.

Layton was a woodsman. His reflexes were as keen as his knife. He sprang as Fargo fell, shearing the razor's edge at Fargo's chest, and it was only by a fluke that the blow missed by the barest fraction.

Fargo got his hand on his Colt and the Colt clear of his holster. A foot caught him on the wrist, numbing it, and the Colt went flying. Inwardly cursing his clumsiness and sluggishness, Fargo rolled to the right and came up in a crouch, his hand sliding into his right boot and groping for the Arkansas toothpick he always carried strapped to his ankle.

Layton did not allow an instant's respite. He thrust his blade at Fargo's chest, then sprang back in surprise when Fargo swept the toothpick up and deflected the stab with a metallic *ching*. Eyes narrowing in wary calculation, Layton bent at the waist in a knife fighter's posture and circled.

Fargo did likewise. It was rash to talk in a fight, any fight, but he did so now. "If you kill me, the judge and Draypool might be upset. It will spoil their plans." He did not add "whatever those plans were."

"I have no choice. You know too much," Layton responded. "We'll still have your body, and that's the important thing."

"My body?" Fargo wondered what in hell that meant.

"You're not as clever as you think," Layton said. "You have no idea what we need you for. It's sure not to track, not when we have Hiram Trask." Layton snickered. "The only thing you're good for is being a convenient scapegoat, as the judge calls it. When your body is found near his, everyone will jump to the wrong conclusion."

"*That's* why I was hired? To take the blame for killing someone I don't even know?" To Fargo it still made no sense.

"You don't know who the man is or you would understand," Layton said. "Everyone will be so busy trying to figure out why you would do such a thing, they won't suspect the League."

"Who are you after?"

"That would be telling."

Without warning, Layton attacked, wielding his knife in a flurry, seeking to overwhelm Fargo quickly. But Fargo was expecting it, and he met the whirlwind with all the considerable skill he had acquired, the clang of steel on steel ringing loud and sharp. He was forced to give way, but only for a few yards. Then he planted himself and would not be moved. He countered or evaded every stroke, every feint. Fury crept into Layton's countenance and he redoubled his effort, but now it was Fargo who forced him back, step by step, until they stood where they had started, both of them swearing and Layton panting as if he had just run ten miles.

"Damn you! No one has ever lasted this long!"

"I intend to last longer," Fargo assured him.

"Think again," Layton said, and clawed for his revolver. He had it half out when Fargo's shoulder slammed into him and they pitched backward into the fire. He stabbed at Fargo's neck but cleaved empty air.

Fargo gained his feet first. He lashed out with his right foot and Layton's Remington sailed into the dark.

"Enough is enough!" Layton growled. He was growing desperate, and he proved it by throwing himself recklessly forward, his knife arcing right and left.

Fargo retreated. He made Layton come after him, made Layton overextend himself, and at the next wild slash, he drove the toothpick's double-edged blade into Layton's forearm.

Crying out, Layton backpedaled, then stopped and regarded the blood seeping from the wound. He was winded and could not last much longer, and they both knew it. "How about if we call this a draw and you let me take my horse and go?"

Shaking his head, Fargo resumed circling. "You tried to kill me. This ends only one way."

"Bastard."

Struck by a thought, Fargo stopped and said slowly, "Unless—"

"Unless what?" Layton eagerly responded.

"Unless you tell me the name of the man the League wants dead. Do that, and I won't try to stop you from leaving."

Layton straightened, blood dripping from his wrist. "I can't. I took a vow. I pledged to be loyal to the League."

"Is your vow worth dying over?"

"The stakes are. This isn't about you or me. It's about sticking up for what I believe in."

"You've lost me," Fargo admitted.

"The judge calls them 'causes greater than ourselves,' " Layton recited. "I have an obligation to do what is best for everyone, not just for me."

"How is murdering someone good for anyone?" Fargo skeptically asked.

"It depends on who. And it's not really a murder. Not in the way you mean."

The quibbling annoyed Fargo. "What other way is there?" he demanded. He wondered if Layton was stalling to regain his strength.

"Nice try, mister. You're fishing, hoping I'll give it away. But I won't. I've made my decision. I would rather die than betray the cause."

Fargo's puzzlement grew. The Secessionist League was devoted to one cause and one cause only. "All this has something to do with the South?"

Desperation compelled Layton to snarl and recklessly throw himself into an attack yet again. He feinted high but sliced low, his intent to bury his knife in Fargo's groin. But the backwoodsman was not the only one with superb reflexes. Fargo's had been honed in clashes with Comanches and Sioux, grizzlies and wolves. His arm moved like lightning. He blocked the knife, and before Layton could recover, Fargo re-

126

versed his grip on the toothpick and slashed it across the other's throat.

For all of five seconds Bill Layton stood in stunned disbelief. Then he bleated and staggered, clutching at the cut in a vain bid to stanch the crimson spray that moistened the front of his buckskin shirt. "No!" he gurgled. "Not like this!"

Fargo did not move closer. So long as the man lived, he was dangerous. "Who is the League after?"

Layton glared.

"His name," Fargo persisted.

"Go to hell!" The words were spat out in a blubbery hiss matched by the hiss of scarlet.

"You first."

Layton tottered, swore, and fell to his knees. Blood gushed over his lower lip in a thick red flow. He glanced wildly about, as if seeking the Remington, then raised his knife to the star-speckled heavens and tried to shout something, but all that came out of his mouth was more blood and inarticulate sounds. He looked at Fargo and weakly cocked his arm to throw his knife. Life fled, and with a final groan he toppled.

Fargo felt for a pulse to be sure. He searched Layton's pockets and saddlebags in the hope of finding a clue to the League's plot, but there was nothing. With a sigh of frustration, he faced to the southwest and then to the northeast. He had a decision to make. Should he go after Harding and Draypool and the rest? Or should he continue tracking and find out who they were after?

Which would it be?

15

Hour after hour the tracks led Fargo north by northeast. The morning passed and the sun was at its zenith when he came to a river. He heard it before he saw it, heard the unmistakable watery rustle, like a sheet sliding across a bed.

The tracks went right up to the river's edge. There, the killer had sat in the dirt, the impression of his buttocks confirming his lean build. He had removed his shoes and socks. Fargo knew because the tracks to the water were those of bare feet.

The killer had waded right in.

Fargo gazed toward the opposite shore. If the killer could cross at that point, so could the Ovaro. There were no rapids to contend with and the water was not deep.

After so much time in the forest, venturing into the open grated on Fargo's nerves. The whole way across, he scoured the other side for a possible ambush. It was an ideal spot. He had nowhere to take cover except in the water. One shot was all it would take to pick him off. But none shattered the muggy air, and presently the Ovaro stood on a flat stretch of shore and shook, spraying drops every which way.

The killer had sat to put on his shoes and socks, then jogged into the trees. Instead of traveling northward though, he bore east along the river, paralleling it.

Fargo sensed a purpose to the change of direction. Not quite half an hour later he came on a wide trail that saw frequent use. The trail started at the river and wound to the north. Dismounting, he walked to the Sangamon. The spot was a regularly used crossing. In the distance, to the south, was a small town.

Fargo scratched his chin in thought. Why had the killer crossed farther down rather than use the normal crossing? To avoid being seen? Then why come to the regular crossing at all? The answer lay at his feet: the jumble of tracks. The killer's were now amid a maze of others. Anyone tracking him would find it that much harder.

Leading the Ovaro by the reins, Fargo walked the first half mile, to a fork where a small trail angled to the northeast. Fewer people used it, and there were fewer tracks. He had no difficulty distinguishing those he had been following from the rest. Smiling to himself, he climbed into the saddle.

Ten minutes later Fargo passed an isolated homestead. In a corral attached to the large cabin were two horses. Several small children stopped playing to stare. So did their father, who was curing a hide. A rifle was propped against a nearby stump. Fargo lifted a hand in greeting and the man did likewise.

Twenty minutes more, and another homestead. This one was smaller than the first, with no corral and no horses. No children, either, but a woman was hanging wash on a line, and on hearing the clomp of the Ovaro's hooves, she called out, and a man emerged with a rifle in his hands. Again Fargo waved. Again the homesteader raised an arm in acknowledgment.

Cautious but friendly. Typical backwoodsmen.

Over an hour later Fargo came on the next homestead, the smallest yet. A dog tied to a stake barked in warning, and a young man and young woman came out, the woman cradling an infant to her bosom, the man with the inevitable rifle. They smiled, and the young man called out, "You're welcome to light and set a spell if you want!"

Fargo reined across the clearing and stopped. "Mind if I ask you folks a question?" he asked politely.

"Is that all?" the man said. "We don't get many visitors. How about a cup of coffee? My wife makes the best you'll taste anywhere."

The woman blushed and said, "Oh, pshaw."

Fargo wouldn't mind, but he had to push on. "Maybe on my way back. I'd like to know if you saw anyone else go by today?"

"Sure didn't," the young man responded. "But I've been inside mostly, making a cradle for the baby."

"I did," the woman said. "I saw him out the window. It wasn't the usual one."

"How's that?" Fargo asked.

It was the husband who answered. "There's a fella who has a cabin deeper in. We don't often see him, maybe once every three or four months." He looked at his wife. "But it wasn't him?"

"No," the woman confirmed. "About the same height and just as skinny, but this one didn't have a beard and was carrying a rifle, not an ax."

"An ax?" Fargo said.

The husband nodded. "The man who lives past us always has an ax with him. Never a gun, just the ax. Carries it like it's part of him."

Fargo touched his hat brim. "I'm obliged." He reined around, then stopped to say over his shoulder, "Keep your eyes peeled. More men might come by, late today or early tomorrow. Stay shy of them. They're not to be trusted."

"What's it about?" the young man asked in sudden concern.

"I'm not sure," Fargo said. "But I suspect they've already killed one family and wouldn't hesitate to harm your wife and you."

"You should go to the law."

"Without proof there's not much a lawman could do," Fargo said, and gigged the stallion.

"Thanks for the warning, mister!"

Fargo had a lot to ponder. For starters, what was he to make of the fact that the man he was following looked a lot like another man who had a cabin farther in? Could it be the woman was mistaken? That the man she saw *was* the same man, only he had shaved his beard and traded his ax for a rifle? Or was the second man a friend of the first? Or was it something else entirely? Answers were elusive. He had too little information to go on.

The trail meandered interminably into the shadowed depths of the woodland. Birds were everywhere. Squirrels scampered in the upper terrace. Deer that had seldom set eyes on human beings stared without fear.

Once, Fargo spooked a young black bear that ran off grunting and huffing.

It was the ring of an ax that alerted Fargo he was close. Coming to a stop, he dismounted, drew his Colt, and led the Ovaro warily forward. The steady *thunk-thunk-thunk* of the ax grew louder.

The homestead was a work in progress. The cabin was the smallest yet. Many of the trees around it had yet to be cleared. A tall, lanky man with a broad chest was attending to that task, his shirtsleeves rolled up to reveal muscular arms. Every stroke of his ax was powerful and precise. Another backwoodsman, if ever there was one.

The tracks Fargo had been following did not enter the clearing. They veered off the trail into the forest.

Squaring his shoulders, Fargo walked into the open. The man swinging the ax did not appear to notice him. Ten feet behind him, Fargo stopped.

Without stopping, the man asked, "Are you fixing to shoot me, citizen?"

"Put it down," Fargo said.

The tall man turned and regarded him intently but not unkindly. He acted more amused than anything else. "This?" He held out the ax.

"That," Fargo confirmed.

"It would be foolish of me to drop my only weapon while a complete stranger holds a gun on me, wouldn't you agree?"

"You don't have any choice."

"I beg to differ. I can go on chopping, or I can invite you in for some refreshment. I have lemonade. It's not cold, but it will slake your thirst."

"Drop it," Fargo repeated, mystified by the man's behavior.

"Or what? You'll shoot me?" The backwoodsman chuckled. He had an easygoing manner about him. "I pride myself on being an excellent judge of character, and you are not the kind to kill someone in cold blood."

"You take awful chances," Fargo said.

"We take risks our whole lives. Day in and day out we must choose between a course that is safe and a course that is less so. But we can't take the safe course if the safe course is not the right one."

The man spoke so earnestly. Fargo studied him anew; his face was bony and angular, the nose prominent, the ears large, but then the man's head was large, too, large and craggy and stamped with character born of experience. It also mirrored an indefinable hint of sadness. One look at him, and Fargo could not imagine him slaughtering an innocent family. He lowered his Colt.

A smile touched the tall man's lips. "You're not going to kill me, then?"

"I don't know what I'm going to do," Fargo said. "I don't savvy any of this. Why do they want you dead? Who are you?"

"You don't know?" The man placed the head of his ax on the ground and leaned on the handle. "But why should you, unless you have heard me speak, or seen a likeness in a newspaper?" He gestured at the cabin. "My place is a carefully guarded secret. I like to get away by myself from time to time, to go back to my roots, as it were, to spend my evenings reading Shakespeare or the Bible." He paused, then bluntly asked, "Who is it wants me dead?"

"They call themselves the Secessionist League—" Fargo began.

The backwoodsman held up a bony hand. "We will finish this discussion inside. I would be remiss as a host if I did not offer you that refreshment." Without awaiting a reply, he swung the ax to his shoulder and strode toward the cabin.

More perplexed than ever, Fargo twirled his Colt into his holster and followed. There was no hitch rail, but there were several pegs in the front wall for hanging tools and whatnot, and Fargo looped the reins around one of them. The cabin was a single room, sparsely furnished, with the bed over against the rear wall. There was a table with a lantern on it, and a rocking chair. A bookcase was the only other furniture. A black pot hung on a tripod in the fireplace.

"Would you like some of my lemonade? Or I can make coffee or tea."

"I'm not all that thirsty." Fargo stayed in the doorway so he could watch the woods, and the trail. "I don't see a gun anywhere."

The man was about to place his ax on the table. Patting it, he said, "I've carried one of these since I was knee-high to a calf. It is the best tool a man can own."

"You can't drop an enemy at a hundred yards with an ax," Fargo replied.

"I would rather persuade an enemy than slay him. Alive, a man has worth and can contribute to the common good. Dead, he is of no use to anyone." He set the ax down. "But I am willing to concede there are times when that is impossible. Times when an enemy leaves us no recourse but to resort to violence." The sadness in his face became more pronounced. "You have slain quite a few, I take it?"

"More than my share," Fargo confessed. "But I never go hunting trouble. Somehow, it just seems to find me."

The backwoodsman grinned. "In that we are much alike. But with the assistance of that Divine Being who ever attends us, we can overcome any difficulty." He moved to the counter, where a half-empty pitcher of lemonade sat beside a bucket of water. "I am being remiss. I will have your water in a jiffy."

"There's no hurry. I'm not going anywhere." Not until Fargo got to the bottom of the mystery. "You still haven't told me your name." He gave his own.

"How unusual. I seem to recall it from somewhere. What is it that you do for a living, if I may ask?" The man poured water into a glass.

"I work as a scout," Fargo disclosed. "I also guide wagon trains now and then. Sometimes I'm hired as a tracker."

"I see." The man brought the glass over. "Did the Secessionist League hire you to track me?"

"To track *someone*," Fargo said, and briefly related the trail he had followed for the past day and a half.

"Then whoever you tracked is out there right now, spying on us?"

"That would be my guess, yes," Fargo said. "The League wants you dead. They concocted a story about a killer called the Sangamon River Monster and hired me to find him. But all I really am to them is a scapegoat. They intend to murder you and have me take the blame."

"Why you?"

"If I knew that, I'd be a happy man," Fargo said sourly.

"Perhaps I can venture a guess." The backwoodsman

leaned back against the table and folded his arms across his chest. "The nation is on the verge of a conflict that will dwarf all others. We are about to be put to the test of whether right truly makes right. There are those who seek to dissolve the Union. To them, I am their greatest enemy, and they will stop at nothing to destroy me."

"Who the hell are you?" Fargo snapped. The man smiled, and then it hit Fargo—the obvious answer, the only answer, the answer that explained everything the Secessionist League had done. He should have seen it sooner, but it never would have occurred to him that the person everyone was talking about, the person who had the newspapers in a tizzy, the person who was roundly cursed and despised by those who believed the South should be permitted to do as it pleased without interference from the North, the person who was the talk of the country, had a small cabin way off in the deep woods where he went every now and again to be alone. "Abe Lincoln!" he blurted, and took a step back.

"I am he," Abraham Lincoln said. "Honest Abe, many call me. It is a pleasure to make your acquaintance. But I am afraid that my presence has placed you in peril. That man hiding out there—"

"Is not the only one we have to worry about." Fargo cut him off. The others would show up soon, Draypool and Harding and their pack of killers. Their scheme was simple, yet devious. He had been lured like a lamb to the slaughter, to the doorstep of Lincoln's cabin, and now the League would close in and dispose of the two of them and arrange things so he appeared to be responsible. The League, and the South, would not be blamed. But that still did not explain why they chose *him*.

"How many are we up against?" Lincoln asked.

"Ten, counting the one outside," Fargo said.

"Too many. You might be harmed." Lincoln picked

up his ax. "If we can make it across the river, I will summon help. Captain Frank Colter and five soldiers have been assigned to protect me, but I would not let them come to the cabin."

"Colter, did you say?" So Fargo had been right; Colter and Sloane were government men. "We have to get you out of here. We'll ride double on my horse."

"There is only the one trail in and out," Lincoln said. "We should cut through the woods and avoid them."

A nicker from the Ovaro and an answering whinny from off in the trees told Fargo it was too late.

The assassins had arrived.

16

Abraham Lincoln started to walk past Fargo to the door. "I will distract them and you can slip into the woods. This isn't your fight."

"Like hell it isn't," Fargo responded. "They used me. Tried to hoodwink me. One of them even tried to kill me."

A kindly smile creased Lincoln's face. "I do not want you to lose your life on my account. As a favor to me, leave now, while you are still able."

"No can do." Fargo did not see any of the conspirators. They were close, though. Very close.

Lincoln accepted the inevitable with a nod. "Very well. Since I can't prevail on you to save your life, we must work together to save both of ours. The question now is whether we make a stand or try to escape."

The cabin was small, but the walls were thick and would be proof against most pistol and rifle fire. But Fargo did not like being cooped up. The League could burn them out, or sit out there and wait until they ran out of water and food. "Our best chance is in the forest."

"I agree," Lincoln said. "I have spent most of my life in the woods, and I am not without some small skill at surviving."

"Let's go." Without further delay, Fargo was out the door and dashed to the Ovaro. He unwound the reins from the peg and hurried around the side. Lincoln was a few steps behind. Both of them had their gaze glued to the trail. No one appeared. No shouts were raised. Fargo figured that the man watching the cabin had been distracted by the arrival of Draypool and the others. Any moment, and that could change. He was glad when they plunged into the vegetation.

"This way," Lincoln said, striding past on those long legs of his. "There is a trail for a short way."

That there was, thanks to the presidential candidate's daily trips to a stream and back. In less than a hundred yards they stood next to the blue ribbon. On the other side lay untamed wilderness.

Fargo crossed and threaded in among the trees. He did not try to erase their tracks. For one thing, the Ovaro's heavy hooves sank too deep into the soft soil. For another, no matter how well he concealed them, it would not fool a seasoned tracker like Hiram Trask. He would only waste his time, time the League would use to gain on them.

"The vagaries of life never cease to astonish me, friend," Abe Lincoln remarked. "Half an hour ago I was chopping wood, at peace with the world and all around me. Now here I am, in peril of my existence."

"Stick with me. I'll get you out."

"Like glue to paper," Lincoln said. "It has long been my practice to stand by those who are in the right and oppose those who are in the wrong. Much as I do on the issue of secession."

Fargo hoped he would not launch into a speech. "There is bound to be killing," he mentioned.

"I know," Lincoln said.

"Have you ever killed anyone before?" Normally that was the kind of question one man never asked another, but Fargo had to know the extent to which he could count on his companion.

"I am proud to say I have not," Lincoln declared. "Bears and deer and other game, yes, but never a human being. Based on your previous comment, I take it that you are not averse to the task."

"Only when I have to," Fargo clarified. He did not add that he had to do it a lot. "When they catch up to us—and they will—I'll hold them off while you get away."

"We can lose them if we leave your horse behind," Lincoln said. "Is there any chance you would consider abandoning him?"

"Not a chance in hell," Fargo said. The Ovaro had saved his skin too many times. He owed it that much, and more.

"I admire you, sir," Abe Lincoln commented. "You are a man of principle. I wish there were more like you in the political realm." He paused. "Perhaps that is part of the reason the League chose you to take the blame."

"My reputation isn't anything like yours," Fargo said in disagreement. "It's no secret that I'm fond of wild females and wild living."

"And you regard that as a blight on your character?" Lincoln deftly slung his ax across his shoulder. "I read voraciously, Mr. Fargo. I am partial to history, but I will read anything I get my hands on when a history is not available. I have read an account or two about you, sir. Yes, you have a reputation for bawdiness. Yes, the stories are quite lurid. But anyone who reads them perceives that you also have positive traits."

"If you say so." Fargo was listening for sounds of pursuit.

"You have a certain notoriety," Lincoln continued. "Imagine the sensation it will cause if I am found dead, presumably murdered at the hands of the famous Trailsman. The public will wonder why, and many will speculate that I must have done something to deserve it. After all, in those stories, you wipe out evildoers in droves."

In a flash of insight Fargo could see the headlines and newspaper accounts by editors friendly to the Secessionist cause, who would paint him as a valiant frontiersman and Lincoln as a menace that had to be destroyed.

"When you think about it, the League is being quite clever," Lincoln said. "They bury me with dishonor and enhance the South's prestige."

Fargo stopped and held up a hand for silence. Distant voices suggested the League had reached the cabin and found them gone. "Mount up." They might as well ride and conserve their strength.

"I still can't convince you to save yourself?" Lincoln asked. "Very well. But I do this against my better judgment."

Fargo rode as fast as he dared. Low limbs threatened to spill them from the saddle. Brush plucked at their legs. Thickets and logs had to be skirted.

Abe Lincoln cleared his throat. "Might I suggest we circle around to the Sangamon River?"

Fargo saw his point. Once south of the river, they were back in civilization. Lincoln was well known and could marshal help, as well as send for the army. Fargo reined to the east.

"This is a fine state of affairs," Lincoln said with transparent sarcasm. "Here I am, running for the highest office in the land, and I am forced to run for my life from those too blind to see that slaying me only delays the South's day of reckoning. Eventually the slavery issue will destroy them."

"You know what they say. Some folks can't see the forest for the trees."

"An astute observation, given our surroundings. The South has yet to realize that the dogmas of the past no longer pertain. The tides of social progress wait for no man."

"Is that from one of your speeches?"

Lincoln laughed. "No, but I may well include it in my next one. I owe it to the nation to persuade both sides to see the light of reason or we will plunge into chaos. The cost in suffering will be incalculable."

"I wouldn't want to be in your boots," Fargo admitted. It was his experience that, human nature being what it was, most people were too stubborn to admit when they were wrong even when they knew they were.

"To be honest, Mr. Fargo, I would rather the burden did not exist. But wishful fancies do not make difficulties go away. Wisdom is called for, and I can only pray I am equal to the occasion."

At that moment Fargo had never respected anyone more. He was about to say it would be a shame if Lincoln were not elected when new sounds pierced the woodlands—the rapid thud of hooves and the crackle of underbrush. The assassins were much nearer than he had figured!

A tap of Fargo's spurs galvanized the Ovaro into a trot. Like those who were after them, Fargo plowed through the growth, heedless of the peril. But the outcome was a foregone conclusion. The Ovaro was as fine a horse as ever lived, with superb stamina, but they were riding double, in dense timber, and had no hope whatsoever of outdistancing their pursuers.

Suddenly drawing rein, Fargo vaulted from the saddle and handed the reins to Abraham Lincoln. "Keep going. I'll hold them as long as I can."

"I refuse," Lincoln said.

"You sure are a stubborn cuss," Fargo said, and yanking his Henry from the saddle scabbard, he smacked the Ovaro. The stallion hurtled forward. It was all Abe Lincoln could do to stay on.

Whirling, Fargo sought cover. A whoop fell on his ears as he crouched beside a maple. Riders materialized, four of them, spaced twenty to thirty feet apart. They had caught sight of Lincoln.

"There he is, boys! After him!"

Fargo snapped the Henry's stock to his shoulder. He recognized the four—Hiram Trask and Trask's three friends. The tracker and his companions had pushed on ahead. Fargo tried to fix a bead on Trask, but the foliage prevented a clear shot. He shifted his sights to the rider on Trask's right.

A semblance of thunder rose to the sky. The rider shrieked and pitched to the earth.

Fargo shifted toward another rider, but more brush was in the way.

"Take cover!" Hiram Trask bellowed.

Trask and the other two melted into the vegetation. The riderless horse galloped on east. Silence claimed the forest, an ominous quiet pregnant with the promise of more violence.

Fargo's main worry now was that Trask and company would slip past him to go after Lincoln. Removing his hat, he placed an ear to the ground but did not detect telltale vibrations. Staying low, he dashed to another tree, shoving his hat back on as he ran.

Another factor Fargo had to keep in mind was that Draypool and Harding and the rest were bound to show up before long. He must deal with Trask and push on quickly.

The next instant, to Fargo's surprise, the tracker shouted his name.

"Can you hear me? You won't stop us! We've taken vows not to rest until Mr. High and Mighty is maggot bait!"

Fargo had Trask's position pegged. Seventy feet away, to the northwest. He swiveled, yearning for a clear shot.

"We'll make it look like you were to blame," Trask hollered. "But you've figured that out, haven't you? It's why you killed Layton."

Let the man talk, Fargo thought. It was a lapse in judgment that Trask would regret, a mistake worthy of a greenhorn.

"What's the matter? Catamount got your tongue? Answer me if you're not yellow."

Fargo almost chuckled at the Southerner's childish antics. Did Trask really believe he could be goaded into revealing where he was?

"No-good Yankee scum! You and that bastard you're protecting! He thinks he has the right to tell us how to live! But we'll show him! We'll show everyone north of the Mason-Dixon!"

A tiny claw of doubt pricked at Fargo's awareness. Maybe *he* was the idiot. Hiram Trask was no greenhorn. Trask would not shout without good reason, and the only reason Fargo could think of was to keep him distracted while Trask's two friends converged for the kill.

A hint of movement demonstrated Fargo was right. Every nerve tingling, he ducked down. He had nearly fallen for one of the oldest ruses in the hills.

The movement resolved itself into the silhouette of one of Trask's companions. The man was staring toward the maple, not the tree Fargo was behind. Careful not to give himself away, Fargo elevated the Henry's barrel. He was lining up the sights when more movement, at a different spot, gave him cause for consternation.

The last member of the quartet was dangerously close. When Fargo fired, the man would have a clear shot. Fargo had to switch targets. But any movement on his part was bound to be noticed.

Hiram Trask had not shut up. "It doesn't have to be like this! You should be on our side! Or have you worked for the army for so long, you're a blue belly at heart? Work with us! Help us deal with so-called Honest Abe and we'll let you ride off in peace. You have my word!"

Fargo would believe him the day it rained gold nuggets. As slow as molasses, he started to turn toward the nearest assassin, and as he expected, the man spotted him. They both took lightning aim, and it was the Henry that thundered first. The man dropped to one knee.

A leaden wasp nearly stung Fargo's ear as he fed another round into the chamber. He fired as the man took aim, fired as the man keeled to one side, fired at the twitching body.

Two more shots banged. Two slugs cored the trunk next to Fargo with loud *thwacks*. He returned fire. The other backwoodsman stiffened, grabbed at his chest, and toppled onto his belly.

Wary of a trick, Fargo stealthily advanced until he could see the man lying in a spreading red ring. His shot had entered the base of the man's throat and ruptured out the back of the neck. There could be no doubt the man was dead.

Three down, one to go, Fargo tallied. And the last might prove to be the most dangerous.

Hiram Trask had stopped shouting; he could be anywhere.

Easing onto his elbows and knees, Fargo crawled toward a log. He avoided twigs that might snap and crunch under his weight.

Something rustled to Fargo's right. He froze, his finger curled around the trigger. A tense half a minute ensued, until a sparrow flitted from a thicket and took wing.

Fargo resumed crawling and reached the log without spying Trask. Once again he removed his hat. Slowly rising onto his elbows, he peered over the log. He was so sure that Trask was somewhere in front of him that the patter of moccasins behind him registered a few heartbeats too late.

He spun, but Trask was on him. "Die, you Yankee-loving son of a bitch!" he sneered viciously.

A bowie flashed in the sunlight.

17

Fargo threw himself onto his back and thrust his rifle at Trask as the bowie descended. Steel rang on steel. Trask kicked, and the Henry was torn from Fargo's grasp. Palming the Arkansas toothpick, Fargo levered himself erect.

Trask crouched, the bowie held low in front of him. Hate blazed from his dark eyes as he snarled, "You can't save him! If we don't get him, someone else will. The call has gone out!"

"It won't be you," Fargo said.

Hiram Trask sprang. He was ungodly fast. He was also extremely skilled with a blade. It was all Fargo could do to counter a fierce series of stabs and slices. Most men would have died then and there.

Suddenly stepping back, Trask studied Fargo with a measure of newfound respect. "So," he said, "tracking isn't the only thing we are evenly matched at."

Fargo continued to circle, placing each foot with care. He must not make a mistake. His wasn't the only life at stake. So was the life of a man he sensed possessed a genuine spark of honesty. "Killing Lincoln won't change how a lot of people feel about slavery."

"Fool. For the South, there is more at stake than the darkies. States are being told what to do by the federal government. We can't allow that."

Fargo glanced past Trask. As yet there was no sign of the other members of the Secessionist League.

"The government has no right to bully us! Free and sovereign states can do as they please. But your precious Lincoln doesn't agree. Killing that bearded bully will show the rest of the country that we will not give in to the likes of him."

"And might lead to war," Fargo said to keep Trask talking. The Southerner had straightened and seemed more interested in jawing than slaying.

"So? You sound like it would be a bad thing. But war has solved a lot of disagreements." Trask smiled slyly. "Hasn't it dawned on you, Trailsman? We *want* war to break out. There is no doubt in our minds the South will win. State sovereignty will be assured. Slavery will last another thousand years."

"Not if I can help it," Fargo said, even as he lanced the toothpick at Trask's belly. Trask neatly sidestepped and countered with a slash at Fargo's wrist. Fargo jerked his arm from harm's way but lost several whangs on his sleeve. Pivoting, he sheared at Trask's throat, but Trask slipped aside with disconcerting ease.

"Too slow," the tracker said, mocking him. "I expected better."

Again Fargo struck. Again he deliberately slowed his hand a shade, enough to be convincing yet not so slow that Trask would penetrate his guard and kill him. Trask laughed, then waded in. Fargo met him head-on. Trask's eyes widened in fleeting surprise that was replaced by savage determination.

More than their knives flashed and clashed. It was a battle of wills. Fargo and Trask called on all the experience at their command in a dazzling display the likes of which few had ever witnessed.

Sweat caked Fargo from head to toe. He had a few nicks on his arms and one on his legs, but so far he had avoided every death thrust.

Trask stepped back again, breathing heavily, bewilderment giving him pause. "For a Yankee you are damn good."

"For a knife fighter you talk too damn much." Fargo stabbed high, at Trask's neck, and Trask reacted as Fargo anticipated by sweeping the bowie up to block the toothpick. But in midblow Fargo dropped the toothpick from his right hand to his left, and before Trask could react, he sheared the toothpick into Trask's abdomen, the blade angled upward so that it sliced under Trask's sternum and pierced the Southerner's heart.

Blood spurting, Hiram Trask stumbled backward. He looked down at himself, blurted, "I'll be damned!" and died oozing to the ground.

Fargo sleeved his forehead and face, then hunkered and wiped the toothpick clean on Trask's buckskin shirt. Sliding the toothpick into his ankle sheath, he stepped to where the Henry lay. As he picked it up he gazed to the east and wondered how Lincoln was faring.

The next moment, the object of his wonderment strode from the trees, leading the Ovaro. "You are a remarkable individual, Skye Fargo."

"I thought I told you to keep going."

"And desert you in a time of need?" Lincoln shook his craggy head. "I would no more abandon the Union to men like him." He nodded at the still form. "Always stand with anybody who is in the right, remember?"

From the west came the crackle of undergrowth.

"I wish you would reconsider. There are six of them left and they all have rifles and revolvers. All it would take is one stray slug."

"Be that as it may," Lincoln said, "I refuse to run. Every fiery trial is a test of character, whether it be an individual's or a nation's, and I will not sully myself with the brand of cowardice."

Fargo could not squander more time arguing. "Take this, then," he said, and tossed the Henry.

Lincoln had to let go of the Ovaro's reins to catch

it. The ax in his other hand, he arched his eyebrows. "What about you?"

Patting the Colt, Fargo answered, "I have this. Take my horse and find a spot to hunker. When I give a yell, cut loose."

"To think," Lincoln said sadly, "I have managed to avoid taking human life until this day. Hatred always reaps a dire harvest, as our fellow Americans will soon learn to their eternal sorrow." He turned and vanished into the vegetation.

Fargo turned, too, and hiked westward, making no attempt to conceal himself. As he walked he drew the Colt. Five cartridges were in the cylinder; he added a sixth, under the hammer. Twirling the Colt into his holster, he took a deep breath to steady his nerves. He was walking into a lions' den, and the lions were thirsty for his blood.

The League had fanned out. Draypool and Judge Harding were at the center of the line, Bryce Avril and Vern Zeck to their left, Garvey and the last conspirator to their right. They rode with rifles at the ready.

Garvey, the overseer, spotted Fargo first. "Look there!" he shouted, extending an arm. He and the others immediately reined up.

Fargo did not break stride. His arms loose at his sides, he casually walked toward them. He counted on confusion and curiosity to gain him the ten yards he needed. Several more strides and he was close enough. Now it did not matter what they did. Stopping, he grinned. "These woods are swarming with snakes in the grass today. Or should I say snakes in the trees?"

Arthur Draypool did not find it the least bit humorous. "We heard shots. Where are Hiram Trask and our other friends?"

"Burning in hell, where they belong. Lead poisoning and cold steel did them in," Fargo revealed. So did cockiness and carelessness.

"Damnation!" Judge Harding angrily exclaimed. "I thought for sure Trask could beat you. But no matter. The odds are still six to one. You were a fool to march up to us in the open this way."

"Wait," Draypool said. He leaned on his saddle horn. "Abraham Lincoln?"

"Is alive and well." Fargo took pleasure in announcing it. "And he will stay that way if I have anything to say about it."

"You don't," Garvey said.

Draypool sighed. "What if I offer you your life, Trailsman? What if I let you leave with no hard feelings? Would you accommodate us?"

"And make it easier for you to murder Abe? After you lured me here to take the blame for assassinating him?" Fargo laughed in their faces. "Sure. I'll turn my back on him, you mangy bastards, but only after all of you are worm food."

Zeck had his rifle halfway to his shoulder. "Say the word, Mr. Draypool, and he's a goner."

"Not quite yet, if you please," Arthur Draypool said. Then, to Fargo, "Which direction has Abraham Lincoln gone?"

"Do you honestly expect me to tell you?" Fargo marveled. Sometimes the man was too ridiculous for words.

"No, I suppose it was too much to ask," Draypool acknowledged. "In which case we have nothing left to say to one another." He nodded at Zeck. "If you would be so kind, Vern."

Fargo's hand was swifter than the nod. He had his Colt·out before Zeck had the rifle level. Cocking the hammer as he drew, he squeezed off a single shot. The slug cored Zeck between the eyes, shattering his nose and blowing off the top of his skull in a spray of hair, bone, and gore. In spasmodic reflex, Zeck's trigger finger tightened and his rifle discharged into the soil in front of his mount. The frightened animal reared, causing Bryce Avril's horse to shy and throwing off Avril's aim so that his shot whizzed harmlessly over Fargo's head.

The rest were bringing their rifles to bear. Draypool, Harding, Garvey, and the other League member fired an uneven volley, peppering the air with lead. In their haste, they missed.

Fargo darted behind an oak, and flattened. They continued to fire at random even though he was lost to their view. He scrambled south a dozen feet, then west.

"Hold your fire!" Judge Harding commanded. "Can't you idiots see that he has gone to ground?"

"Where did he get to?" Draypool asked anxiously. "Did we hit him? Fan out and find out!"

"No!" Judge Harding bellowed. "We stick together! Avril, watch to the south! Garvey, the west! Clifton, keep your eyes peeled to the north. If a blade of grass so much as moves, shoot at it."

Fargo froze. He had wanted to slip behind them unnoticed, but the wily judge had thwarted him.

"What about Lincoln?" Garvey asked. "Shouldn't some of us ride on ahead and get this over with?"

"Don't worry. He won't get far," Judge Harding said. "We'll catch him long before he reaches the Sangamon."

"What makes you think he'll head for the river?" Arthur Draypool asked.

"Because whatever else Lincoln might be, he's not stupid," Judge Harding said. "His only hope is to cross the river and get help, and he knows it."

Fargo began to replace the spent cartridge in his Colt. In order not to give himself away he moved with painstaking slowness.

"I can't stand just sitting here," Draypool complained. "He can pick us off one by one. At least send Avril into the trees to look around."

"No." The judge was adamant. "Your man is good

at killing, but in these woods Fargo has the advantage."

Their squabbling had enabled Fargo to reload. Facing them, he slid backward until he had gone far enough to ensure they did not see him when he rose into a crouch behind a pine. For all their bluster, the secessionists did not possess much woodland savvy. He aimed at Bryce Avril.

"There!" Avril suddenly barked, and his rifle spat.

Fargo heard the slug bite into the pine. He answered in kind. His shot smashed into Avril's face, dissolving the nose into fleshy pulp. Avril joined Zeck in a prone posture of death.

The others commenced firing, forcing Fargo to drop flat and crab to his left. Bits of vegetation rained down, clipped by the hailstorm.

Suddenly Clifton reined wide of the rest and galloped toward the pine Fargo had vacated, firing his rifle with admirable proficiency. Judge Harding shouted at him to stop, but Clifton did not obey.

Fargo heaved onto his knees and fired twice, fanning the Colt with practiced precision. At each blast Clifton rocked with the impact. His rifle drooped and he swayed. Fargo did not waste another shot. He threw himself flat yet again as the horse thundered by. Clifton's body thudded to the ground.

Three conspirators remained. Fargo had three cartridges left in his Colt. He would rather have more, and went to reload.

"Rush him!" Arthur Draypool bawled, beside himself with fury. "All of us at once!"

"Don't!" the judge yelled.

But Draypool and Garvey charged, firing on the fly. An invisible fist knocked Fargo's hat from his head. Invisible fingers tugged at his left sleeve. Rising onto one knee, he shot Draypool squarely in the chest, then had to leap aside as Garvey nearly rode him down. Garvey twisted in the saddle and fired as Fargo fired, not once but twice. The bottom of Garvey's jaw exploded and the overseer fell.

The Colt was empty. Fargo whirled, his hand flying to his belt. The *click* of a rifle hammer—and the muzzle trained on him—turned him to stone.

Judge Oliver Harding smiled. "Any last comments?"

Fargo was a statue.

"No? You gave a good accounting. I'll give you that much. But it's over. You've lost. As soon as I put an end to you, I'll go after Lincoln."

"That won't be necessary."

The voice came from so near that both Fargo and Judge Harding gave a start. A familiar lanky frame came out of the shadows into the sunlight, as inviting a target as anyone could ask for.

"You!" Judge Harding exclaimed. "I didn't think you would make it so easy." He drew a bead on the presidential candidate.

Fargo had to act. Only a few feet away lay a fallen rifle. In a bound he reached it and swept it up. He fired without aiming, as much to rattle Harding as anything else. The judge shifted toward him. Both of their rifles boomed.

The judge missed.

Fargo did not.

Abraham Lincoln came over and placed a hand on his shoulder. "I am forever in your debt."

"It's not over," Fargo said. "There's a man named Mayfair I plan to visit. He's part of the League."

"Let the army deal with him," Lincoln suggested. "I will have Captain Colter take him into custody. With the help of Providence, we will uncover the rest of their sinister organization."

"Whatever you think is best."

Abraham Lincoln smiled warmly and offered his hand. "Can I count on your vote come the election?"

Grinning, Fargo shook. "I don't usually bother. But in your case I might make an exception."

High Plains, Kansas Territory, 1860—
where Judge Lynch presides and
Fargo is invited to a social—a hemp social.

Skye Fargo stood in the shadow beside his hotel room window, keeping a wary eye directed outside on the ramshackle livery barn at the far edge of town.

Since entering the Kansas Territory three days earlier, he had been followed by two young Southern Cheyenne bucks. Because most Plains Indians were partial to pinto horses, and Fargo rode a top-notch pinto stallion, it seemed likely they meant to boost his Ovaro.

Cheyennes, he knew, were not town fighters. Sneaking into a livery in broad daylight, however, to steal a white man's mount would count as a great deed and earn them coup feathers. So Fargo had slid open the sash and had his brass-framed Henry rifle propped against the wall nearby. He had no intention to shoot for score, only to kick up plenty of dust and send the braves running.

Fargo wore fringed buckskins, some of the strings stiff with old blood. His crop-bearded face was tanned hickory-nut brown, and the startling, lake blue eyes had seen several lifetimes of danger and adventure. He cast a wide glance around the once-thriving town of Plum Creek.

"Boom to bust," he muttered, amazed by the rapid change.

The last time the Trailsman, as some called Fargo, rode through Plum Creek, the place was fast and wide open. Seemed like everybody had money to throw at the birds. But he had watched plenty of boomtowns turn into ghost towns practically overnight, and clearly this berg would soon make the list. Last night a rough bunch of buffalo skinners had made enough ruckus to wake snakes. The hiders were gone now, and the sleepy little crossroads settlement seemed on the verge of blowing away like a tumbleweed.

There was still this hotel, though, Fargo reminded himself, even if it was the size of a packing crate. And even more surprising, a bank straight across the street. That was especially hard to believe—Fargo had played draw poker the night before with a few locals, and all but one had used hard-times tokens as markers, private coins issued by area merchants to combat the critical shortage of specie.

Again Fargo's gaze cut to the livery, but the Ovaro was peacefully drinking from a water trough in the paddock. Fargo watched sparrow hawks circling in the empty sky. The only traffic in the wide, rutted main street was a despondent-looking farmer driving a manure wagon.

Until, that is, a fancy-fringed surrey came spinning around a corner near the bank.

Fargo whistled appreciatively when he'd gotten a good look at the driver. "Well, ain't *she* silky satin?" he asked the four walls of his cramped room.

The surrey pulled up in front of the bank in a boil of yellow dust. The Trailsman forgot about the two Cheyennes, dumbfounded at this vision of loveliness. The young woman on the spring seat was somewhere in her early twenties with lush, dark-blond hair pulled straight back under a silver tiara and caught up under a silk net on her nape. Hers was a face of angelic beauty except for full, sensuous lips.

Fargo had an excellent view, and with his window open he heard everything that transpired.

"Yoo-hoo, young man!" she called out in a voice like waltzing violins. "Yes, I mean you. Come here, please."

A slight, puzzled frown wrinkled Fargo's brow. Her accent, he guessed, was supposed to sound French and might fly in these parts. He'd heard better imitations, though.

A boy of about twelve years of age, a hornbook tucked under his arm, was just then passing along the raw-lumber boardwalk. At the woman's musical hail, he turned to look at her and his jaw dropped open in astonishment. Like Fargo, he seemed mesmerized by the gay ostrich-feather boa draped loosely around slim white shoulders, and the way her tight stays thrust her breasts up provocatively.

"Yes, you," she said again, laughing at his stupefaction. "I don't bite!"

"Hell, a little biting might be tolerable," Fargo muttered.

"Please run inside the bank," she told the awed lad, taking a coin from her beaded reticule, "and tell them an invalid lady requires help outside."

"Yes, muh-muh-ma'am!" the kid managed, staring at the coin she placed in his hand.

Invalid? Fargo's eyes raked over her evidently healthy form. It was early September—dog days on the High Plains—and the still air felt hot as molten glass. Yet, the mysterious woman's legs were wrapped in velvet traveling rugs.

Fargo's vague suspicion of the beauty instantly deepened. He was familiar with the ways of grifters, and it didn't take him long to twig the game. No traffic outside, the bad French accent—and her noontime arrival when only one teller, probably the bank manager, would likely be on duty. Suddenly he recalled one of Allan Pinkerton's detectives telling him about how the "beautiful invalid" scam worked with surprising ease at small-town banks. Gallant managers were eager to run outside and cash small bonds or redeem stock coupons, leaving the bank briefly unoccupied.

Sure enough, one dashed out now, resplendent in pomaded hair, a new wool suit, and glossy ankle boots.

"Your servant, Madame," he greeted her, even tossing in a clumsy bow.

"*Now* I see which way the wind sets," Fargo muttered, a grin touching his lips.

The sheep was about to be fleeced, but the Trailsman had no intention of stepping in just yet. This was going to be a good show and Fargo, mind-numbed by his long ride across the plains, needed the diversion. However, he resolved to recover and return the money later—the citizens of Plum Creek were poor as Job's turkey and could ill afford a loss. Besides, that course of action allowed him to see the woman up close. In this territory, females like her were only seen in barroom paintings of Greek and Roman nymphs.

"Sir, you are *so* kind!" the striking young woman effused. "I have been in your wonderful country for only six months, and I am—how you say?—puzzled about bonds. May I ask a few no-doubt silly questions?"

"Madame, *nothing* you ask could be silly," the bank officer assured her.

Fargo shook with mirth while the deceitful shill, as he assumed her to be, removed some papers from a wallet. As the two conferred, heads intimately close together, Fargo watched behind them for the woman's partner. Yet, even knowing what was coming, Fargo's eyes were almost deceived.

The sneak thief was impressively adept at swift, silent movement. Like a fast shadow he glided out of an alley and onto the boardwalk, soundless in the cork-soled shoes of his trade. He slipped inside the bank so quickly that eagle-eyed Fargo hardly gained an impression—only that the small, dapper man's hair was silver at the temples and his fox-sharp face slightly puffed and lined.

"And what is this," the woman's lilting voice inquired, "about ac-cum-u-la-tive interest? *Ciel!* Such a difficult word!"

Fargo laughed outright, admiring the little sharper in spite of her criminality. Right now, while the bedazzled bank manager stood in a stupor, the sneak thief inside would spend less than two minutes rifling the open vault. If the vault was closed, or yielded little, he would leap to the cash drawers. Then he would unlock the rear door and make his escape.

The moment the woman reined her two-horse team around and headed back out of town, Fargo went into action.

He buckled on his heavy leather gun belt and

palmed the cylinder of his single-action Colt to check the workings before he snatched up his Henry. He trotted down to the livery, tacked the Ovaro, and swung up and over, reining in the direction of the surrey's dust trail.

Not surprisingly, the conveyance was making jig time as the couple tried to avoid capture. For the Ovaro, however, it was swift work to carry Fargo alongside. The "invalid" was no longer driving, that job falling to her male partner. Keeping his eyes on both, Fargo leaned out and grabbed the reins from the man, drawing back to halt the team.

The beauty's nostrils flared in anger. "Sir! I protest! My father and I are in an urgent hurry!"

Fargo, grinning like a butcher's dog, let his eyes sweep over her. "Well, pardon me all to hell. Sweetheart, you really need to polish that phony accent. Sounds like you got a bad head cold."

"Phony?" she protested. "It is the way we speak in Par-ee, but, *mais oui,* of course a benighted savage like *you* would not know this."

Fargo took in wide emerald green eyes with thick lashes that could flutter most men into total submission. She had flawless skin like creamy lotion, a figure that would tempt a saint to impure thoughts—and Fargo was no saint.

However, the Trailsman was forced to shift his attention to her companion, whose right hand was inching toward his vest. The man was compact and well-groomed, in his forties, with distinguished silver streaks in his hair, a neat line of silver mustache, and shrewd, intelligent eyes that missed nothing.

His hand moved another inch and Fargo said mildly, "Don't miscalculate yourself, mister. Just because I'm smiling politely don't mean I won't kill you if you skin that hideout gun. Real slow, toss it down."

"Now see here!" he protested in a suave baritone, his accent as phony as the woman's. "I am merely checking the time. See?"

Under Fargo's close scrutiny he slid a watch from the fob pocket of his silk vest and thumbed back the cover. "*Mon Dieu!* We are indeed tardy for our appointment, Arlette. Sir, my daughter and I have a crucial engagement and must resume our journey."

Fargo laughed. "Damn straight you must. The sheriff of Plum Creek is hard as sacked salt. Maybe you've heard of the Kansas troubles? This whole region is known for hemp socials, and 'trials' take place a few minutes before the hanging. Even for genteel bank robbers like you. True, even here they won't hang a woman, but *you* will decorate a cottonwood."

"Bank robbers! How preposterous! We employ neither masks nor guns, the tools of that nefarious trade."

"If it chops wood," Fargo assured him, "you can call it an ax. You talk like a book, mister, and I don't trust flowery men. Now shuck out that hideout gun, nice and easy."

The girl calling herself Arlette tossed back her pretty head and laughed, showing Fargo even little teeth white as pearls. "*You,* sir, are in my bad books," she coquetted.

Fargo knew it was just a desperate bid to distract him so her companion could get the drop on him. Fargo's Colt leaped into his fist. The loud click, when he thumb-cocked it, made both grifters go a shade paler.

"Cottontail, you can play that bank manager like a piano, but I know women like he knows ledgers. Now, mister, hand it over, and don't try a fox play or I'll let daylight through you. That's something I'd surely hate to do, by the way."

The man's veneer of cool composure now cracked

completely. Scowling, he handed Fargo a two-shot derringer with a folding knife under the barrels.

"Now," Fargo added, "hand over that buckskin pouch that's on the seat between you."

"Sir," the man protested, his face going red with anger, "yours is the manner of a man who holds the high ground and all the escape trails. *If* we stole this money, as you boldly assert, how are you any different from us? Clearly you intend to steal it for yourself."

"The hell you jabbering about?" Fargo said, growing impatient—he thought he spotted dust puffs from the direction of town. "You're lucky I'm letting you two ride on instead of turning you over to the law. Now hand over that swag and get going before I change my mind."

"You hairy brute!" Arlette flung at him. "Neanderthal! Picking on gentlemen and ladies must be your specialty!"

Fargo laughed again, glancing inside the pouch before tucking it into a saddle pannier. He tapped both bullets out of the derringer and tossed it into the surrey.

"No need to get on your high horse, missy," he said. "All I steal are kisses. By the way— both of you seem to be losing your *French* accents."

Arlette blushed to her very earlobes as the man, suddenly cursing out Fargo like a dockworker, removed the whip from the surrey's socket and lashed the team into motion.

Fargo headed back toward Plum Creek and quickly realized his mistake—the bank robbery had been discovered almost immediately because that was definitely a posse thundering right at him. He had figured to return the stolen money before the alarm was raised. Banks never reported a robbery if they could recover the money without publicity.

Possibly, a witness had seen him leave town in a hurry. The Plum Creek sheriff, Hinton Davis, had kept a wary eye on Fargo last night, and Fargo saw him pocketing payoffs from the town's few remaining sporting gals. He didn't strike the Trailsman as a by-the-books lawman. And the "good citizens" with him right now, Fargo realized with a sinking heart, looked more like a hemp committee than a posse. He recognized several scurvy-ridden toughs who had been in the saloon last night.

"Well, old campaigner," Fargo said to the Ovaro, "looks like I put our bacon in the fire again."

The moment he fell silent, still trying to decide what to do, the whipcrack of a rifle sent ice into Fargo's veins. That first shot hissed wide, but within seconds more bullets hummed like blowflies past his ears, some so close he felt the tickle of wind-rip.

The moment of stunned immobility passed in a blink, and the will to live instinctively asserted itself. He still had a full magazine in his sixteen-shot Henry, and six beans in the wheel of his walnut-gripped Colt. This was no time, however, to make a stand. That jackleg posse was coming at him like the devil beating bark, and clearly they had no plans to arrest him. Nor was Fargo willing to kill any of them—after all, it was his legal duty to report, or stop, the bank theft, not let it play out for his amusement.

"Fargo, you damned knucklehead," he cursed himself as he clawed the buckskin pouch from his pannier, "I hope you enjoyed your little diversion."

However, he didn't toss down the pouch as he'd intended. Fargo knew that Davis and his minions would give up the chase quickly once they had the money. The initial excitement would be over, and they were townies. However, Fargo also believed this bunch would split the swag, not return it to the bank.

He would send it back to Plum Creek by express rider first chance he got.

Fargo reined the Ovaro around, kicked him up to a gallop, and lowered his profile in the saddle. Fearing for the two grifters, he veered off the road and led the vengeful pursuers toward more rugged terrain, bullets thumping the ground all around him.

No other series has this much historical action!

THE TRAILSMAN

GRITTY HISTORICAL ACTION FROM

USA TODAY BESTSELLING AUTHOR

RALPH COTTON

Available wherever books are sold or at
penguin.com